JIM

THE
BANANA
SMUGGLER

Poo

DEDICATION

This book has to be dedicated to my wife Moo, who, despite having to endure long periods of silence while I write, has encouraged and supported me throughout and shares in my success.

ACKNOWLEDGMENTS

Cover illustrations by the brilliant artist and graphic designer Dan Lowe

www.airfieldstudio.com

Inspiration provided by my two wonderful Grandchildren, The Princess Maggie and Sir Vince-a lot.

ONE

In the Palace, the Prince was sitting on a large open veranda looking down over his garden of lush green palm trees and shrubs beyond which he could see the harbour and beyond that the Currybean sea. He was the Prince of the Island of Grenana and he loved his island. It was beautiful, very green and always sunny. His people were happy and showed their love for him by clapping and cheering whenever he passed. But in reality, he was a mean spiteful little man that would scream and shout if he didn't get whatever he wanted. His people smiled and waved when he passed just to avoid his tantrums.

Cook appeared carrying a plate of banana sandwiches. He had bought a massive bunch of bananas from the market but had bought too many. The staff were all eating them, the guards were all eating them, some had been sent to the army barracks and some out to the Navy, and he still had loads left.

He placed the plate on the table and smiling gave a little bow as he stepped back. The Prince looked at the plate, looked at the cook and then back to the plate. He snarled as he turned over a corner of one of the sandwiches. 'Banana's again. I had bananas yesterday, and the day before,' then with his voice rising, 'and you dare to bring me bananas again.' He stood up with the plate in his hand. Cook backed away. 'But your Majesty,' he began to explain. 'We have so many, and they are good for you, and we need to . . . ' 'I don't care,' the Prince shouted. 'I don't want bananas. I'm sick of bananas. I don't like bananas anymore.' His eyes fixed the cook with a steely stare and cook knew what was coming. Screaming 'Fetch me something else,' the Prince angrily hurled the plate through the air.

Poor cook instinctively started to dodge the flying plate but then froze in fear of what the Prince might do if it missed. He caught the plate, squashing the contents against his tunic and with the Prince continuing to scream he turned and scurried out.

He ran down the corridor burbling 'Oh what to do? Something else, something quick.' His fingers were shaking and that gave him an idea. 'Fingers. Yes fingers. He likes fingers. I'll go to the harbour. Find a fisherman. Get some fingers. Yes. Fish fingers.' Cook ran as fast as he could, out of the palace and down towards the harbour.

Jim was busy selling his bananas in the market. He had persuaded cook to buy the massive bunch a few days before. Jim saw cook running from the palace and as he hurried past gave cook a nod with his head. 'Trouble. Trouble. The Prince has gone off bananas,' the cook called out as he passed.' The people around Jim's stall gasped and everybody muttered. 'Gone off bananas. The Prince has gone off bananas. What could that mean?' Jim watched as the cook disappeared into the harbour. 'Trouble,' he said.' This could mean trouble.' He thought for a moment. 'I think I might need to make some plans before I come back.'

A week later Jim was back in the market. He had spoken

to the palace cook, the cooks in the army barracks and the cooks on the navy ships and they all agreed that it would be better if they all bought their own bananas. That way everybody would still get their bananas and the poor palace cook wouldn't end up with too many. The only person that wouldn't get any would be the Prince. A good plan Jim thought.

In the palace the Prince stood on his veranda looking down on the harbour where his new flagship laid waiting for his inspection. His butler placed his robe over his shoulders and walking to the courtyard he climbed into his state carriage and with his horse guard assembled front and rear. The procession set off.

Jim heard the commotion as the procession approached the market. It was the Prince who gave people permission to trade in the market and Jim wasn't sure how the Prince would react if he saw a cart full of bananas. But Jim was prepared, he quickly pulled a tarpaulin over his cart to cover his bananas. As the Prince passed, he noticed Jim and gave him a severe look. But Jim was clapping and cheering just like everybody else and there were no bananas. The Prince was appeased.

The procession rolled into the harbour and alighting from his carriage the Prince stood on the quay side proudly surveying his new ship. With its tall masts and pristine rigging it looked magnificent. He had had it designed and built by the best naval architect to catch a pirate that had been active around the island recently.

He walked up the gangplank and onto the deck where the Admiral bowed gracefully as he welcomed him onboard. He had just been promoted and given command of this fine new ship and was nervous to impress the Prince. 'Would you like to inspect the crew your Majesty.' He beckoned the Prince towards very straight lines of men looking very smart in their new navy uniforms. The Prince walked along the lines inspecting each man to make sure he was correctly turned out. Satisfied he turned to the Admiral, 'Well done Admiral. Now I would like a grand tour of the ship.'

The Admiral showed the Prince around the ship. Every deck was scrubbed, every canon blacked, every fitting polished, every knot and rope perfect. 'That pirate will have no chance against this ship your Majesty,' the Admiral boasted. 'He won't dare come into our waters knowing we are here, and if he does, we'll catch him in no time.' The Prince agreed. He had the best ship, the best Admiral and the best crew. The pirate would have no chance.

At the end of the tour the Admiral took the Prince to the poop deck where some tables had been laid out. 'We have prepared some lunch for your Majesty.' The Admiral gestured the Prince towards the tables. The Prince was pleased, he was starting feel a little peckish. He stepped forward looking forward to something to eat but as he reached the table his smile disappeared, his eyes hardened and his lips curled. 'What, is, this?' he said angrily.

'Bananas your Majesty.' The Admiral explained. 'The ships cook went to market and bought them fresh this morning.

You can have them with some bread, honey, cream or custard or just by themselves.' The Admiral gestured towards the food again but instead of picking up a sandwich the Prince's eyes went wild and flying into a rage he angrily grabbed one side of the table and flipped it over, 'BANANAS. YOU WANT TO FEED ME BANANAS. I DON'T WANT BANANAS. I'M FED UP WITH BANANAS. I DON'T LIKE BANANAS.' He paused fuming, the table now upside down and its contents scattered all over the deck. 'This morning you say. From the market you say.' He remembered seeing Jim. Turning to the Captain of his guard he snarled his instructions. 'Send some men to the market square. Find that rascal Jim and remove his permit. Throw him out. He is no longer allowed to sell his wretched bananas on my market, or anywhere else in the town.'

The Captain sent a sergeant with six men. It didn't take them long to reach the market and they knew exactly where Jim would be.

Jim saw people moving aside as the soldiers approached and knew immediately it meant trouble. He slipped sideways behind the stall next to him and then again behind the one after that. He slipped easily through the people in the market and by the time the sergeant reached his cart Jim was hidden, rolled up in a carpet by one of the other traders. The sergeant stood by Jim's cart and looked around. 'Where is he?' he demanded of the traders close by. They all just shrugged their shoulders. 'I think he's gone for a wee,' one said. The sergeant ordered his men to search the market and the local inns. As they searched one stood at the end of the carpet where Jim was hidden. Jim dared not to breath in fear of the carpet dust making him sneeze. The soldier moved on and Jim stayed well hidden.

After searching without success the sergeant stood with his men at Jim's cart. 'By order of the Prince,' he shouted. 'Bananas can no longer be sold on this market or anywhere else in the town. The trading permit held by Jim has been cancelled. He is to be thrown off the market. Any person knowing his whereabouts must come forward immediately.' He waited for a short while looking around at the traders but nobody moved.

Turning to his men he gave a loud order. 'These bananas are confiscated and will be taken and destroyed. Men, pull that cart and follow me.' As they left the market he gave his men a quieter order. 'Take these bananas to the barracks. Tell the cooks these are the last. We might never get anymore.'

The market traders watched the soldiers leave before unrolling the carpet to free Jim. 'Tough luck Jim,' they all said. 'What will you do now?' Jim stood still as the sergeant's words raced round his head. Not being able to sell his bananas meant no money to buy other things. 'I don't know,' he said. 'I really don't know.'

Leaving the market and the town Jim trudged through the jungle muttering to himself as he made his way back to his plantation. 'Nasty little man. Nobody else can have bananas just because he doesn't like them anymore. And stopping me from making a living. I need to do something. But what?' He knew not to make decisions while he was angry and he was very angry. But he couldn't stop his mind and plans and alternative plans kept racing through his mind. By the time he got home he had decided what to do.

TWO

Over the next few weeks Jim made preparations. He walked for many miles through the jungle that surrounded the town. He picked his places and then he was ready. But first he had to go into town to visit some friends.

Jim walked out of the jungle and across the fields where the islands food was grown. Field workers were busy tending to the produce and apart from a few that stopped to gave him a wave, nobody took any notice. But as Jim went through a town gate he was stopped by some soldiers. The sergeant walked around Jim looking him up and down. 'Well well well. Who have we here? You know you're not allowed to sell your bananas anymore and we have instructions from the Prince to make sure you don't.' Jim held his hands out, palms up. 'Do I look as though I'm selling bananas. Where do you think I'd hide them.' The sergeant looked at Jim suspiciously. Jim was wearing just a tea shirt and shorts. There was no sign of any hidden bananas. 'Go out to the jungle where he's just come from,' the sergeant ordered some of his men. 'Make sure he hasn't hidden any bananas out there.'

They waited while the men went out and searched. Shortly after they came back. 'Nothing,' they said. 'No bananas anywhere.' 'Very well,' the sergeant said. 'You can go. This time. But we're watching you.'

Jim walked into town and through the streets. He was aware that there was always somebody following him. Watching, making sure he didn't get up to any tricks. He knew many people in the town and would stop often to shake hands and exchange greetings. He went into the market and chatted with his old friends; all the while aware that he was being watched. He bought some provisions then set off back the way he had come.

'Bye sergeant,' he said, giving the guards at the gate a little wave as he passed. He walked out into and across the fields grinning, trying hard not to laugh. 'He's up to something,' the sergeant said to his men. 'Wait until he's across the fields then we'll follow him. Find out what he's up to.'

As soon as Jim reached the jungle the guards raced across the fields. They paused briefly then followed the path Jim had taken. 'Keep your eyes peeled lads,' the sergeant whispered. 'He's up to something.' Jim heard them coming and watched as they went past, carefully hidden in some undergrowth. He knew they would follow him. He had deliberately tried to look as though he was up to something, which he was. Just not what the soldiers thought. He waited a short while before emerging. He looked along the track where the soldiers had disappeared then shaking his head muttering 'stupid boys' turned around and went the other way.

Early next morning back on his plantation he loaded his carts with bananas and set off. Reaching a small jungle clearing just outside the town he climbed a tall palm tree and tied a green flag with a big yellow X to the top of the trunk. This was the signal to let people know where he was. It didn't take long before there was a steady stream of people coming and going and Jim was sold out before the end of the day. 'This is a good plan,' Jim thought chuckling to himself. 'He said I couldn't sell my bananas in the town. He didn't say I couldn't sell them anywhere else.'

Jim was thoughtful and knew that the Prince would be angry if he found out what he was doing. He continued his jungle banana trade for a number of weeks, each time moving to a different clearing to stop the soldiers setting a trap or him. His old customers all knew to look for his flag and apart from not being able to trade in the town, things seemed to be going pretty well.

Some weeks later the Prince was conducting an inspection of his army's barracks. With the captain of the guard close behind he inspected the troops on the parade ground. He inspected the barracks to make sure all the beds were correctly made and the floors were clean and shiny. All seemed well. The next part of the inspection was the kitchen. As the Prince entered, the cook was preparing lunch. The Prince came to a sudden stop just inside the door, the captain almost bumping into him. The Princes eyes went wild not believe what he was seeing. The kitchen staff were peeling bananas, lots of them.

'Captain,' the Prince shouted. 'What is this. I told you to throw Jim off my market, out of my town and ban him from selling bananas.'

The Captain came forward. 'Yes your majesty. It was done. His permit was cancelled, his bananas confiscated and he knows he can't sell bananas anymore.'

'Then **where** have these come from,' the Prince gestured towards the bananas. Turning to the cook who was now beginning to tremble the Prince demanded, 'Where did you get these bananas?' 'F f f f ffrom the banana sale your Majesty,' the cook stammered. 'In the jungle. He sells them in the jungle. All we have to do is look for his flag to know where he is.'

The Prince's eyes narrowed. 'So! He thinks he can sell them without my permission does he. Captain. Find that rogue and arrest him. Throw him in the dungeon. Make sure the people understand, the sale of bananas is forbidden anywhere on this island.'

A few days later Jim was busy selling bananas in a jungle clearing. People were coming and going guided by the flag. The Captain stood on the town wall watching. He had sent the sergeant and his men through a different gate further away to creep through the jungle. He knew the people would warn Jim if soldiers were seen walking through the fields towards him.

Jim was doing brisk trade and there was a queue of people at his cart all wanting bananas. The soldiers had been very careful and crept through the jungle without a sound. Jim was unaware of the eyes peering at him through the undergrowth. A shout of 'NOW' rang out, soldiers suddenly emerged from the jungle and before Jim could move he was surrounded. The sergeant stepped forward clearing the people out of the way. He smiled as he looked at Jim, pleased he had caught him. In a very loud and clear voice he called. 'The Prince has decreed that the sale of bananas is forbidden anywhere on this island. Jim, you are under arrest and will be thrown into the palace dungeon.' This was serious. The palace dungeon was only used for really bad people and was not a place Jim wanted to visit. He had to think fast.

A quick look round at the soldiers surrounding him told him that there was no chance of escape. The people in the clearing were starting to leave, some with bananas and some without. A sudden spark in Jim's head lit up his mind, 'But sergeant. What about all these bananas,' Jim said. 'We can't just leave them here. We might as well let the people have them, and your men.' 'I don't know,' the sergeant said rubbing his chin. 'My orders are to . . .' But the people had heard Jim and were turning back. In a few seconds they were crowding round Jim's cart beginning to clear it of bananas. 'You'd best be quick,' Jim said to the sergeant's men. 'There'll be non-left in a minute.' The sergeant's men quickly joined in and within seconds the people and soldiers were all pushing and shoving round the cart all trying to get some bananas. 'You'd better take control of this sergeant,' Jim said urgently. 'They'll be fighting in a minute.' The sergeant could see the danger and stepping forward shouting orders soon had an orderly queue formed so that everybody would get a fair share. He turned back to deal with Jim, but Jim wasn't there. Using the confusion Jim had quietly slipped back into the jungle and was nowhere to be seen.

'Oh no!' The sergeant said realising that he would never find Jim now. He was going to have to go back and tell his Captain and the Prince that Jim had escaped. He closed his eyes and took a deep breath. He would be in big trouble.

Jim made his way through the jungle and back to his plantation shack. 'I can't stay here,' he realised. 'They'll come looking for me.' He quickly gathered some things together and disappeared back into the jungle. It was easy to hide in the jungle when you knew how. He built himself a shelter using jungle branches and leaves and settled down.

Over the next couple of weeks he heard soldiers searching but he kept himself well hidden. One day while he was dozing under a bush he woke to hear soldiers all around him. They were beating about with sticks and some were coming directly towards him. He froze, he would be seen if he tried to escape. Slowly and carefully he lifted a large broad leaf under which he had dug a pit to hide his belongings. Sliding into the pit he let the leaf down and waited, not daring to breath. He heard the swish of a stick as it passed over the spot where he had just been sitting and was relieved as the soldier moved on. He spent the rest of that day hiding in the hole, thinking. 'That was too close for comfort. I can't let that happen again, and they'll be coming back this way again.' With the idea that they wouldn't search an area twice and being careful not to leave any trace of where he had been he moved his camp into an area the soldiers had searched earlier. Every day the soldiers passed by on their way to a new search area.

As weeks went by the searches became less and less frequent and Jim was getting worried about his trees.

Without the right care he would lose bananas and new trees wouldn't grow. One quiet day he crept back to his plantation and remaining hidden in the undergrowth looked around carefully. Some trees were bearing ripe bananas and some had bananas that had already gone brown. He could see some soldiers wandering around, searching for any sign that he had been there. A few even picked some bananas and put them in their back packs.

He heard voices close by. 'He hasn't been here corporal. No sign of him and nothing's been disturbed. He must have given up or died in the jungle.' 'Perhaps, and perhaps not,' the corporal replied. 'The most we can say is that we can't find him, but that doesn't mean he's gone.' The corporal looked around at the trees and dense undergrowth surrounding Jim's plantation. 'Jim is smart. He's out there somewhere. He could even be watching us right now and we wouldn't know. But he won't get into the town or sell his bananas like before. The captain's made sure of that, and he wouldn't dare to come back here. Come on, lets go.' Jim watched the soldiers leave and waited a while before creeping out to pick some bananas for himself.

Back at his camp he sat wondering what to do. He was an outlaw now. He couldn't sell his bananas in the town or on the island. He couldn't even live on his plantation. One evening as he dozed off to sleep a plan slowly began to form in his head. He tossed and turned all night with all kinds of crazy ideas worming and mingling in his mind but when morning came and Jim woke up, he knew. 'That's it. That's what I'm going to do. I have a plan'

THREE

Jim sneaked back to his shack to get some tools and materials and spent the next couple of weeks in the jungle measuring, sawing, hacking, hammering and banging and before not too long it was finished. He was almost ready but first he had to go into town to tell everybody what he was doing. He was feeling quite pleased with himself. 'This is a good plan,' he thought.

He came out of the jungle and crossed the fields that surrounded the town. People were working, tending crops, picking melons, berries and other fruit and veg. Nobody took any notice of Jim until he got to the town gate. Guards were checking everybody that passed through. 'Good Morning,' Jim greeted the corporal as he was stopped. Morning Ma'am,' the corporal replied, looking at Jim a bit unsure. This was the ugliest woman he had ever seen. 'I haven't seen you round here before. Where have you come from and where are you going.' Jim smiled and did his best to look demure in his home made dress. He hid as much of his face as he could behind his gloved hand and the long hair of his wig. In a very gruff female voice he replied, 'Oh no corporal. You won't have seen me. I used to live in the town. I was a cook in an inn and I never came out of the kitchen. But I'm retired now, I have a little place just outside of town. I've just come in for a few supplies.'

'OK,' the corporal replied, still not sure. 'Have you seen anything of the outlaw Jim?' For a moment Jim thought he had been discovered, then the corporal continued.

21

'He's out there somewhere and he's a wanted man.' 'Oh no corporal,' Jim replied trying to sound surprised. 'Not a sight nor sound.' Then in the most bashful voice he could manage, 'But if I do, I will be sure to come and tell you.' The corporal became a little afraid. He didn't want to encourage any further contact with this woman. 'OK. On you go.' The corporal and his men watched as the woman walked into the streets. 'I hope I've never eaten anything she's cooked,' one of his men said. 'Me too,' said another. 'I feel sick,' another joined in. 'Enough.' The corporal ordered. 'Back to work. We're here to make sure the outlaw Jim doesn't come through these gates.'

Many people gave Jim some very strange looks as he wandered through the streets. He stopped to talk to a few here and there where after a few moments of astonishment there were bursts of laughter. Jim made his way to the market where the same thing happened. 'I see lots of soldiers on patrol,' Jim said to one of his old friends. 'Yeh. They've really stepped things up since you escaped and disappeared. That sergeant's a corporal now.' 'Yeh I know,' Jim laughed. 'I met him again as I came through the gate.' They chuckled then his friend continued. 'They have guards at all of the gates. They patrol the streets, the walls and even the jungle around the town. They think you're out there somewhere and are making sure you can't setup shop again.' 'That's fine,' Jim said. 'They'll be looking in the wrong place.' Jim explained his plan and after he had wandered around the town making his preparations he went back to the jungle.

Every day the guards patrolled the streets and town walls, looking for any signs that Jim might be selling bananas. On the town wall the Captain was addressing some of his men. 'Keep your eyes open men. Look for any flags flying or anybody carrying bananas.' 'Perhaps he's decided not to sell bananas anymore,' one of the men said. 'Perhaps, but I doubt it,' the Captain replied. 'I've known Jim for many years and he's not the kind of man who gives up. He's up to something.'

As he spoke his eyes fell on a small boy in the street below. He blinked slowly to make sure his eyes weren't playing trick on him. 'Banana,' he said pointing. 'That child's eating a banana. Quick. Catch him.' The soldiers ran along the wall to the next set of steps but the child had seen them. By the time the soldiers got to where he had been all that was left was a banana skin on the floor. 'Search everywhere. Find him,' the Captain ordered. His men ran along streets and down alleyways. They looked everywhere but the boy was nowhere to be found. 'Do we tell the Prince,' one of his men asked. 'No. We have to catch him first. If I tell him that Jim's in the town somewhere selling bananas and I didn't catch him he'll demote me. He's here somewhere and we need to find him.'

The Captain sent his men in all directions searching everywhere but they found no sign of Jim. Then a woman was spotted pushing a cart along the beach path just outside of town. Moving quickly the soldiers soon surrounded the woman and stopped her. Next to her was a small boy. 'What have we here,' the Captain said as he pulled back the sheet covering her cart. 'Wood! You have

23

a cart load of wood?' 'Yes. Driftwood for my fire,' the woman replied. 'But not just wood,' the Captain said carefully lifting a few pieces. 'You also have some not very well hidden, B A N A N A S.' 'Oh. Eh. Yeh. I forgot about those,' the woman tried to explain. 'There was a man, in a boat, in Shallow Bay, and it's been such a long time since we've had any. And my boy so wanted some.'

'Quick men,' the Captain shouted running towards the bay. 'We have him now.' The soldiers ran but as they reached the bay all they saw was the tip of a sail as it disappeared round the point. At the helm Jim was smiling. His plan had worked well but as he sailed away he was unaware that he'd been seen.

The Captain made his report to the Prince. 'I have discovered Jim's plan,' he proudly announced. He didn't mention anything about the child eating a banana, the woman, the dash to the bay or not catching Jim in the act.

A week later Jim returned with another load of bananas. He anchored in the bay and waited. He had let the people know when he would be back and it didn't take long for the first person to come into sight. Then another and another. They appeared at various points around the bay. 'That odd,' thought Jim. 'They should be coming from the same direction.' Then he noticed that one was wearing a uniform and another. They all were. Oh! This isn't good.' Jim thought. 'Time to go.' Jim had chosen shallow bay so that people could wade out to his boat, but so could the soldiers. They entered the water and began to converge on Jim.

24

But Jim had a plan. Jim always had a plan. He knew that soldiers wouldn't be able to move quickly through the water and this would give him time to escape. He slowly pulled up his anchor and tipping all of his bananas into the bay he hoisted his sail.

As the wind began to push him out to sea Jim laughed to himself, his escape plan had worked very well. But as he left the soldier behind and sailed round the point he was confronted by a huge shape. The Princes flag ship had been waiting. Jim quickly turned his little boat around trying to get away but as hard as he tried it wasn't long before the great ship loomed above him. Shortly after he was stood on the deck facing the Prince.

The Prince was pacing up and down. Smiling smugly, looking at Jim. 'So. You thought you could defy me did you? Thought you could make a mockery of me did you?' Jim watched the Prince intently and knew he was in big trouble. 'Oh no your majesty,' he responded, 'I would never do that. You said I couldn't sell my bananas in the market and I stopped. Then you said I couldn't sell my bananas on the island, and I stopped. I would never disobey you your majesty.' Jim was trying hard to appease the Prince. 'Then what are you doing here?' The Prince asked angrily staring at Jim. 'You're still selling bananas'. 'Yes, but, I'm not ON the island your highness. I'm OFF the island, in the bay, OFF the island.' Jim gestured towards the bay and smiled. 'Just as you ordered.'

The Prince gave Jim a long hard stare before he spoke again. 'You knew what I meant. I meant no bananas on my island and there will be no more bananas on my island.'

The Prince paced up and down for a while, thinking. 'You have made a fool of me,' he said. 'And the people have seen this. I must make an example of you. The people must see that I will not be made a fool of.'

Turning to the Captain of the guard he gave his first order. 'Captain. Take as many men as you need to Jim's plantation and chop down all of his banana trees.' 'But your majesty.' Jim tried to protest. 'There's years of work there. My father and his father all worked hard to build that plantation.' I don't care', the Prince retorted. 'No bananas on my island. The people must know that when I give a command I mean it.' He looked at Jim, rubbing his chin. 'But what to do with you. You must be punished and the people must know that you've been punished.' He stopped to think. 'I could put you in my dungeon but I don't want you in my dungeon, sooner or later I will have to let you out. The punishment needs to be permanent.' Jim was suddenly afraid. What did permanent mean? The Prince looked over the side of the ship. Was the Prince going to make Jim walk the plank? 'I see you have built yourself a small boat.' He turned to the Admiral and commanded. 'Take him out there.' He pointed out to sea. 'Out there, for many, many many, many many many miles. Over the horizon, over the next one and over the one after that. Put him in his boat and leave him there.' Turning back to Jim he solemnly said, 'Jim from this day forward you are banished from my island. You may never return.'

After a short visit to the harbour to allow the Prince and his guard to go ashore the flag ship set sail for the horizon. The Prince watched from his veranda as the ship disappeared into the distance. He didn't smile. In a small way he admired Jim for the determination and ingenuity he had shown. But Jim had disobeyed him and made him look a fool. The people had to know that he was a strong Prince and the punishment had to be severe. He turned away. His aides were waiting for him to deal with other issues. The Jim problem had been resolved.

On the ship, sitting on the deck with irons round his ankles Jim was wondering what was going to happen. Where would they leave him? Where would he go? Would he even survive?

FOUR

A few days later Jim was in his small boat watching as the flag ship sailed away. The Admiral had given him enough food and water to last for a couple of days but not enough to get back to the island in his small boat. 'Keep going north,' the Admiral had said. 'There are some islands to the north. You should be able to get there.'

Jim set sail and headed north. He sailed all day and all night. Then all day again and all night again. When he needed to sleep he pulled his sail down and slept under it. He kept scanning the horizon for some sign of land but all he saw were rolling ocean waves. Jim began to worry and began to ration what was left of his food and water. Another day and another night and still no sight of land. Perhaps the Admiral had lied. Jim worried, he had no plan for this. Then something caught his eye on the horizon. He wasn't quite sure what at first but as the thing got closer he recognised it as a sail. 'Oh yes!' He shouted in utter relief. 'They've come back for me.' He watched as the sail got closer and closer still then waved as hard as he could until it was close enough for him to see the flag. 'Oh! A Scull and Crossbones.' Jim said to himself. 'This might not be so good.'

The lookout on the pirate ship had seen Jim and soon the ship was coming to a stop close to Jim's boat. The pirate stood on the poop deck looking down at Jim. In a great drolling pirate voice he shouted down to Jim, 'You seems to be in a spot of bovver.' Jim stammered a reply. 'Ah, yeh. I was cast adrift. I'm a banana farmer. I don't have any treasure.' 'Arr yes. Oy heards abowt that. An if you ad any treasure you wouldn't be owt ere in a totty little bowt loyk that. Come ons up. Oy'll takes you to laand.'

Jim climbed the sides of the ship and was met on deck by the pirate. 'Your not going to cut my throat?' Jim asked nervously. 'No, no Jim lad. I dozn't do that. Oy steals treasure but I dozn't cuts throwts. Unless I dozn't loyks you. Then I moyt.'

Even as the pirate was speaking Jim was looking round at the ship. 'Do it look familiar?' the pirate asked. 'Yeh.' Jim said a bit puzzled. 'A lot like. . . .' 'The Princes new flag ship,' the pirate finished for him. 'Yeh. But how? The Prince had that ship designed and built by the best navel architect. To catch you,' Jim said with a little laugh. 'Arr yes. Oy knows all abowt that. That ship will never catch this one. This ship's a lot farster than his poyle of old wood. An oy can sayls this ship all by meself.'

Jim couldn't believe what he was hearing. 'How? How have you managed to get a better ship than the Prince.' 'Becaase Jim lad,' then changing to a very posh refined voice, 'the architect that designed his ship was non other than myself.' Jim was speechless. It was a moment or two before he could utter. 'What? You! You're the architect that designed the Princes ship.' 'Indeed I am. Jeremiah Keel at your service,' the pirate said while giving Jim a very elaborate bow.

Jim roared with laughter. 'Oh my, Oh my,' he eventually muttered. 'The Prince employed you to design a ship to catch yourself. I couldn't make this up.' Jeremiah smiled widely then explained. 'I used to do a bit of pirating in an old ship I had spare. Just as a bit of a hobby you understand to make sure everybody kept their navy's up to date.

Then the Prince came along and demanded that I build him the best ship in the world to catch the pirate. So I did. Then after delivery he decided not to pay me in full. I couldn't believe it. Arrogant little man. I couldn't let him get away with that so I built this, with many improvements on his. This really is the fastest ship on the ocean.' Jeramiah looked around his ship with obvious pride. He looked up at the rigging and shouted. 'Monkey. Come down and meet our new friend.' There was a screech from the top of the mast and a small figure leapt out from the crows nest and with a few very neat leaps from mast to rope and mast again was sitting on the pirates shoulder. 'This is monkey. He's been with me for a while now. Bit of a pest at times but he's learned to look after the top rigging and he's a very good lookout. Or he would be if I could understand anything he screeched. But when he does screech at least I know there's something wrong. All I have to do is figure out what.'

Sending monkey back to his post they set off. 'What are you going to do now?' Jeremiah asked Jim. 'I don't really know,' Jim said. 'I'm banished from the island, I have nowhere to live so I suppose I'm homeless now.' Jeramiah looked at him. 'You can stay on my island,' he said.

It took them another two days to reach the secret island where Jeramiah had his base. On the way Jeramiah begun to teach Jim how to sail the ship. 'You're a fast learner and not a bad sailor for a banana farmer,' Jeramiah complimented Jim.

They came into the secret bay and after tying up the ship, Jeramiah showed Jim around his island. 'Nobody else lives here,' he said. 'There's just jungle, beaches, lots of palm trees and my shack. Not much to do I'm afraid.' Then switching back to his pirate droll, 'but you can cums owt an elps me when I goes owt poyritin.' Jim laughed. 'Maybe. I need to do something but poyritin isn't really my game.' He looked at the ground where they stood and crouching down examined the soil. 'This is very good soil,' he said. It would be perfect for growing bananas. But even if I could, there's nobody to sell them to.'

'Oh, I'm not so sure.' Jeramiah said thoughtfully. 'I know the islanders aren't very happy that they can't have anymore bananas. And if you could grow some here we could take them to Grenana in my ship. I'm sure you'd find a way to sell them. What would you need?' Jim thought or a few moments. 'I would need to get back to my plantation.' 'But what for? They've chopped all your trees down.' 'I need some tools and equipment. They might have chopped my trees down but the roots are still there. All I need are some roots, I can grow new trees from the roots, it only takes nine months. All I need is to get there.' Jim and Jeremiah sat and made some plans. 'We could go straight into the harbour as a trading ship Jeremiah said. They wouldn't take any notice of a trading ship. But we need to get your tools and roots onto the ship, and that might attract attention.'

A few days later they were at sea. Jim was at the helm and

monkey was on lookout. We'll make a wide loop below the horizon so they don't see us and come in from the other side. I know a nice little bay close to the volcano where we can anchor. They won't be looking for you anymore so we should be alright.'

A few days later, with the ship at anchor, they rowed ashore. Jim was pleased to be home but sad that he wasn't allowed to live there anymore. Trekking through the jungle they reached Jim's old plantation. Jim went into his old shed and brought out lots of buckets, tools, equipment, some carts and even some of his old clothes. 'I'll need all of this,' he said. He looked at what was left of his trees, laid on the ground surrounded by dead leaves. Clearing the way to where he needed to be he dug down. He took cuttings from the roots and placed them in the buckets with some soil. After loading them and the tools and equipment onto the carts they were ready to go.

'Oo Oo. Ee Ee. Ah Ah.' Monkey suddenly screeched, pointing. 'Somebody's coming.' Jeremiah said quietly. 'Come on quick.' They quickly pulled the carts into the jungle. 'Keep going,' Jim said. 'I'll catch you up.' Jim went back, quickly covered their tracks then made some deep footprints to the other side of the plantation and into the jungle. Then running round the edge of the plantation, being careful not to leave track this time, he soon re-joined the Jeremiah and monkey. They quickly disappeared deep into the jungle, Jim covering their tracks as they went. 'You're a crafty so and so,' Jeremiah said. 'I like to have a plan ready, just in case,' Jim replied.

A platoon of soldiers arrived at the plantation. They had a

quick look around and settled down for a rest. 'It's a shame there aren't any bananas here,' one said. 'I'm hungry.' 'That's enough of that lad.' The corporal said. 'Bananas aren't allowed, for anyone. Those are the Princes orders.' As he spoke his eyes fell on a patch of newly dug soil. 'What's this,' he said jumping up. 'Somebody's been here. Quick, check the shed.'

The soldiers quickly searched Jim's old shed. 'There's nobody here now corporal but somebody's been here. Carts and equipment and some of Jim's clothes are gone.' 'He's back,' the corporal said. 'Corporal. Over here,' one of his men was shouting. 'Some tracks, going into the jungle.' 'Follow those tracks,' the corporal ordered his men. 'Search everywhere. Find him.'

'They must be sending patrols to the plantation,' Jim said as they rowed the supplies out to the ship. 'They'll know I've been there. They'll find the digging and see that stuff's gone.' 'I wouldn't worry about that now,' Jeremiah said. 'We've got what you need. All you have to worry about now is growing some new bananas.'

FIVE

In the palace the Captain was making his report to the Prince. 'He's definitely been there your Majesty. The corporal reports that carts and tools have gone, and it look as though he's been digging for something. Perhaps roots.' 'Why didn't you destroy everything when you chopped his trees down,' the Prince asked. 'Because we thought he was gone forever your Majesty.'

The Prince pondered. 'He must have turned his boat around and somehow made it back. He must be planning to start a new plantation somewhere on the island. Captain. I am forming a new guard. It will be called the Special Banana Guard, The SBG, you will be at its head.' The Captain stiffened to attention. 'Yes your majesty. Thank You.' 'You will search this island from end to end. 'He must be here somewhere. Find him and bring him to me. He will not grow bananas on my island.'

For months the SBG searched the island. They searched through the jungle, along the shore and around the lava flows at the base of the volcano. But there was no sign of Jim's new plantation. Everyday the Captain would report to the Prince and everyday the Prince would scream and shout at the Captain for failing in his duty.

Meanwhile, many miles away, Jim had been very busy. His new trees had been growing and new bananas were beginning to form. 'It won't be long now. He announced to Jeremiah. 'I think it's time we visited Grenana to make some arrangements.'

Over the last few months Jeremiah had taught Jim how to handle the ship and how to navigate. They had made a couple of trips to Buba, where Jeramiah had his dockyard, and they had sailed past Grenana several times. 'Never go straight there and never straight back,' he had taught Jim. 'Always come from a different direction. That way we're always just another trade ship going past, and If they do ever realise it's us, they won't be able to work out which direction our island is in.'

A few days later, Jim carefully steered the ship into the harbour on Grenana. Jim, Jeremiah and the ship were disguised as traders. Deciding that it was just a bit too hard to disguise a monkey, monkey had been told to stay out of sight. As they tied up, the harbour master came to meet them. They explained that they had come to meet some merchants and set up new shipping deals and after completing the formalities they went ashore. Jim and Jeramiah had not lied. They did meet several merchants and did make deals and soon everything was set.

As they untied to leave the harbour master came back. 'Nice to see you again,' he said smiling at Jim. The shock on Jim's face was all too obvious. Had he been discovered. 'Don't worry. Your secret's safe with me,' the harbour master said, tapping the side of his nose. 'Just don't make it obvious and I'll make sure you get waved through. I'm looking forward to having some,' he looked around before finishing his sentence, 'bananas.'

'I thought my disguise was better than that,' Jim said to Jeremiah as they sailed away. 'Your beard's slipped,'

Jeremiah said. 'You might need to grow a real one.'

Some weeks later they returned. With the ship berthed safely in the harbour, several long crates were unloaded and stacked on the quay side. A soldier from the Special Banana Guard came along to inspect the cargo. The harbour master tried to get the cargo through without inspection but the guard was having none of it. The harbour master looked worried as the guard walked up to the crates. 'What have we here,' the guard asked. Jim saw the concern the harbour masters face. 'Cloth,' Jim replied quickly. 'Cloth from Buba.' Everyone held their breath as the guard prised one of the crates open and looked inside. All he saw were bales of cloth. 'Very well. Carry on,' he said, satisfied that all was well.

The crates were taken to several different warehouses in the town. Jim and Jeremiah followed. Over the next two days each crate was opened and the top layer of cloth removed to reveal the bananas below. People came and left with little bundles wrapped in cloth. As soon as the bananas were sold the crates were returned to the ship, all but one was empty. The guard looked inside. 'Why are you taking these back,' he asked, looking at bales of cloth in the crate. 'Rejects,' Jim explained. 'We have to take any rejects back to Buba to get them exchanged.' In reality it was cloth they hadn't used to wrap bananas that they would need for the next trip.

In the palace, the Captain of the SBG was making his

report to the Prince. 'Still no sign of him your Highness. And no sign of any bananas.' 'He's here somewhere,' the Prince said walking towards the veranda. As he stood thinking, he noticed a ship leaving harbour. 'But if you can't find him here, he must be somewhere else. What's that ship?' 'It's a merchant ship your Highness. Selling cloth from Buba. One of my men checked it yesterday.' 'Ok. Stay vigilant Captain. He's up to something. I can feel it in my bones.' They both stood, watching the ship as it sailed away. 'It couldn't be,' the Prince said. 'No,' the Captain replied. 'Where would he get a ship like that?' 'Indeed. Where?' the Prince replied deep in thought. A little way out to sea the ship turned to port and disappeared round the headland. The two men stood watching, suspicions aroused. 'I'll order my men to make a sweep of the streets and search some houses. Just to be sure.' 'Yes Captain, do that. Just to be sure.'

The Captain called the SBG out of their barracks and began a search of the town. They searched streets, warehouses, the market, houses and kitchens but the people soon realised what was happening and word spread faster that the guards could search. The guards found no bananas. The people had them all very well hidden.

The Captain stood with his men on the corner of the market. The search had revealed nothing but he was uneasy. 'Something's not right,' he muttered. His mind wandered as his eyes looked around and as he looked down to a pile of rubbish something caught his eye. He reached down and picking up the object held it out. His men gasped. A banana skin. 'I knew it.' The Captain shouted. 'I knew it. He has been here.' He looked towards the harbour. 'Who searched that ship?' he asked. 'I did sir.' One of his men said stepping forward. 'I didn't search the whole ship. Just looked into one of the crates.' 'And what did you find?' 'Cloth sir. Just bales of cloth.' The Captain thought or a moment. 'And did we find any cloth during our searches?' No sir. No, we didn't.' The Captain smiled. 'So it was him. That's what he was up to. He'll come back and try the same trick. But we'll be ready. Next time we'll be ready.'

SIX

Some weeks later Jim and the Jeremiah were returning to Grenana. They had sailed in a big loop over the horizon and were approaching the island from a different direction. As they got closer they passed a few of the Princes navy ships. 'They're not looking for traders,' Jeremiah said as they sailed past. They be lookin for a poyrate ship,' he said, slipping back into his pirate droll. 'An there be no poyrates rown dear.' They both laughed.

As they approached the island Jim scanned the harbour through the telescope. 'There's no ships in the harbour. The navy's all out to sea.' 'Strange,' Jeremiah replied. 'There's usually one or two in there. They might be out on exercise.' Jim turned his telescope to a tall tree on top of a hill. 'No,' he said. 'Keep going. Don't turn towards the harbour. They're not on exercise, they're out to try and catch us.' 'How do you know that?' Jeremiah asked, looking at Jim in surprise. 'Because there's a red cloth in the top of that tree. I arranged for a signal to warn us if the Prince found out what were doing.' Jeremiah smiled, 'You are one crafty man,' he said. 'I had a plan,' Jim replied. 'I like to have a plan.'

In the palace the Prince and the Captain were watching from the veranda as the ship got closer. The Prince was getting excited. 'Ha ha. Straight into our trap. Ships at sea to surround him and soldiers in the harbour to catch him. We'll soon have him.' As the Princes excitement grew he began to jump up and down. But then instead of turning towards the harbour, the ship sailed by. 'What. What. What's going on? What's going on? Captain, where is he going? Where is he going? Quick. Send a signal. Send a signal to the Admiral. Tell him to catch that ship. He won't escape my flag ship,' he said, finally realising that Jim wasn't going to fall into the trap.

On the balcony, a sailor began to wave a series of flags. These were seen by a sailor on the harbour wall who began to repeat the signal to another out on the point, who in turn began to wave his flags frantically to a ship out at sea. 'Signal from the shore sir,' a sailor shouted to the Admiral. 'It says that the ship that has just passed the harbour is the smuggler. We are to catch it.'

But it had taken precious minutes for the signal to reach the Admiral and Jim's ship was now sailing past between the flag ship and the island. 'Hoist all sails,' the Admiral ordered. 'Catch that ship.' He was confident he would catch it, after all, he had the fastest ship on the sea.

'The flag ships hoisted his main sails,' Jim said looking behind. 'No matter,' Jeremiah replied. 'He won't catch us.' Standing behind the big wheel that steered the ship, he opened a door to a new secret compartment and pulled a lever inside. Big flaps on the sides of the ship opened and great booms swung out then up to form extra masts. Rigging swung out from the booms and then sails unfurled and filled with wind. 'What's this,' Jim shouted. 'Jeremiah laughed. 'A slight modification. We were already faster than him but I thought we might need a bit of extra speed at some point. Now's as good a time as any to test my new sails.'

'Get ready men. We'll soon catch him.' The Admiral shouted to the crew who were getting ready to board Jim's ship. But instead of getting closer, Jim's ship was getting further and further away. 'What? Not possible. He's getting away. Hoist more sail. Go faster,' the Admiral shouted to his crew. 'We can't hoist anymore sail sir. It's already all up,' one of the crew called back.

Jim watched as the distance between the ships got greater and greater. He called out to Jeremiah. 'Steer a course for the other side of the island. Sail close to the shore where we went for the roots.' 'What are you up to?' Jeremiah asked. 'I have a plan.' Jim said. Jim always had a plan.

Jim lifted the crates out of the hold and assembled them on deck. He had already painted them blue. He took the bales of cloth out, leaving only one. He quickly tied the crates together, end to end. 'Pass as close to the shore as you can, then once I'm off turn out to sea. I'll need monkey to give me a hand. Come on monkey'. As they passed close to the shore Jim opened the gate in the handrail and gave the first crate a big shove. Over the side it went. Then he shoved the second and third and fourth until there was enough weight to pull the rest behind. Jim and monkey jumped onto the last crate as it went over the side. 'Come back for me tomorrow evening.' Jim shouted to Jeremiah as he splashed into the water. Jeremiah swung the big wheel that steered the ship and turned out to sea. As he pulled away the flag ship came back into view. 'There he is,' the Admiral shouted. 'After him.'

Jim laid on the last crate with monkey. The blue crates

were very low in the water and almost impossible to see. They watched as their ship disappeared, followed by the flag ship and several smaller navy ships. As soon as he thought it was safe Jim began to paddle as was soon ashore. They pulled the crates across the beach and into the jungle. After clearing their tracks in the sand they hid the crates under some big jungle leaves.

Monkey looked at the crates and wondered how they were going to get them to town. 'Oo Oo Oo eek Aah.' He said. 'I don't know what your saying monkey, but whatever it is don't worry. I have a plan.' Jim always had a plan. Leaving the crates well covered they walked towards town. Arriving at a spot in the jungle, Jim uncovered a parcel he had left hidden. Later that day an ugly woman was seen walking through the town, stopping every now and then to talk to people. Soon everything was organised, tomorrow was going to be a big day.

Next morning the Admiral was explaining to the Prince why they hadn't caught the banana smuggler's ship. One of our sails was torn,' he lied. We couldn't get up to top speed so we couldn't catch him, but we chased him away. He won't be able to bring his bananas ashore now.' 'Mmm,' said the Prince. 'Perhaps not this time but he will try again. We will have to be ready. Anyway, I didn't want to have to deal with him today. Today the islanders have organised a family walk around the island, and a picnic in my honour.' He puffed his little chest out. 'It's really great that they honour me in such a way.'

In the town the people were gathering. Families and

groups of friends all ready for a great day. The Prince watched as the great procession set off. He wouldn't be joining them on the walk but would be attending the great picnic at the end of the day. A route had been marked round the island for everyone to follow and soon there was a long line of people all walking, talking, telling jokes and children playing as they made their way. It was a great day. After a while they began to pass the place where Jim had hidden his crates of bananas. Some people began to disappear into the jungle, only to re-emerge shortly after carrying a small bundle wrapped in cloth. And so the great procession continued.

Towards the end of the day people began to gather on a beach close to the town and a great party began. The Prince walked through the crowds, waving his royal hand to the people who bowed, curtseyed and cheered as he passed. 'They love me,' he thought to himself. 'This great party in my honour. Oh how they love me.'

As he strolled through the crowd a ship came round the headland and headed out to sea. The Prince looked and shook his head. 'That can't be,' he said. 'Captain. Tell me. That can't be.' 'No your majesty. The Admiral chased him out to sea yesterday and the people have all been on your walk today. He couldn't have.'

The next day soldiers of the Special Banana Guard were making a routine patrol of the island. They came to the spot where the great picnic had been held. The islanders had been very good and taken all of their rubbish home. But here and there, there were odd bits of litter that had been missed. 'Pick these bits up.' The corporal ordered his men. 'We don't want to spoil our island.' The men spread out and began to pick the remaining litter when one pulled at something that had been partially buried in the sand. 'Corporal,' he said holding it up. Another soldier had also found something and did the same. And then another. It would seem that some children didn't understand the instruction from their parents to take all rubbish home and had simply buried their banana skins in the sand.

Later the corporal stood with the Captain of the Special Banana Guard as he reported what he had found to the Prince. 'WHAT! WHAT! UNDER MY NOSE. UNDER MY VERY NOSE. THEY DARED TO EAT BANANAS UNDER MY VERY NOSE. GO. GO NOW. ARREST THEM. ARREST THEM ALL.' 'But we don't know who your Majesty. The whole island was there. We can't arrest them all.

The Prince fell silent realising that Jim had made a fool of him once again. The Captain was worried. The Prince might demote him for not stopping Jim. 'They mock me,' the Prince muttered. 'My own people mock me.' He looked at the Captain but before he began to speak the Captain quickly explained. 'I have doubled the guard in the town,' your Majesty. 'I have given orders to stop and search anyone carrying seen bundles or looking suspicious and ordered the spot searching of houses and kitchens. Anyone in possession of a banana will be arrested.'

The Prince gave the Captain a really hard stare. He had been about to demote him but it seemed that the Captain had already taken action. 'Very well. Very well. But if he gets anymore bananas onto my island'. . . . . He waved his finger at the Captain, and the Captain understood

SEVEN

Jim and Jeramiah zig zagged across the sea making sure they hadn't been seen and weren't being followed. 'It'll be harder next time,' Jeramiah warned. They know what the ship looks like now and they'll be watching for us.' 'I know,' Jim replied. 'It's a pity we can't disguise the ship in some way. We could keep giving it different names. That might fool them.' 'The ship doesn't have a name,' Jeramiah said. 'Never got round to it.' 'Yeh, I noticed the name plate was blank,' Jim replied thoughtfully. 'How about the Jolly Nana. That would be a good name and we could change the name plate whenever we go out banana smuggling.' Jeremiah laughed. 'I like that,' he said, 'but I think it will take a bit more than a name change. We need to change the whole shape of the ship.'

They arrived back on the secret island and made the ship secure. As they entered the shack Jim noticed a large envelope on the table. 'I thought nobody else knew about this place,' he said. 'Only one other,' Jeramiah replied. 'My man in Buba. He brings me messages sometimes.' Jeramiah opened the envelope and read the contents. 'Sorry Jim, we'll have to put banana smuggling on hold for a little while. Some important things have come up and I'm needed back in my office. You can come with me if you like. Might as well use the opportunity to put the ship in the dock yard and get some work done.'

After spending a day or two tending to his trees they

loaded two crates full of bananas onto the Jolly Nana and set off. It was a four day trip to Buba, the biggest island in the Currybean Sea. They pulled into the dockyard where they were met by the yard manager. Jeremiah gave him some instructions then he and Jim left, Jeramiah to his office and Jim to the market with the crates. Jim had taken a few bananas to give to people on the previous trips to see if they liked them. This time he was going to try to sell some.

Meeting up with Jeramiah at the end of the day Jim happily reported, 'It seems that my bananas are a big success on Buba. I've sold them all.' 'Well done,' Jeremiah said. 'Why don't you give up on Grenana and just sell them here.' 'I'd thought of that,' Jim said, 'but the people on Grenana are my friends. They like bananas and I don't want to let them down. And not to go would mean the Prince has won, and I really really don't want to let him win.' A broad smile spread across Jeramiah's face. He perfectly understood Jim's desire not to let the Prince win. 'We can do both,' he said. 'You can set up a business here and we can still make trips to Grenana, just for the fun of annoying that arrogant little man.'

They stayed on Buba for a couple of weeks. The work on the ship was complete and Jim was getting anxious to get back to tend to his trees. 'I'm sorry Jim but I still have lots of work to do here,' Jeremiah told him. 'I'm going to be a few more weeks. You can take The Jolly Nana back if you like. You can handle her now and you know how to navigate. I just need to show you some of the modifications.'

Next day Jeramiah stood on the dockside waving Jim and
monkey away. He and Jim had become good friends and
Jim had become a very good sailor. He knew the Jolly
Nana was in good hands. With Jim at the helm and
monkey on lookout at the top of the middle mast they zig
zagged across the sea, just in case any of the Princes ships
happened to be on patrol this far up. Eventually they
arrived safely back on the secret island and Jim spent a
number of days tending to his trees. 'I've got a lot of
bananas almost ready for sale.' he said to monkey. 'It's too
early to go back for Jeramiah so I think we might make a
trip to Grenana.' 'Oooooo,' monkey replied.

After loading the ship they set off. The sails billowed as
the wind pushed him ever closer to Grenana. With the
sun high in the blue sky and his hands shielding his eyes he
scanned the horizon. 'Monkey,' he shouted. 'Can you see
anything from up there?' One loud screech came down
from the top of the middle mast which in monkey
language, Jim hoped, meant no. He was on his own now
and keeping a sharp lookout for the Princes ships.

On Grenana the Prince was pacing up and down on his
veranda. 'WHY HAVEN'T YOU CAUGHT HIM YET,'
He was shouting to the Admiral and the Captain of the
Special Banana Guard. 'He is only one man, in one ship,
and he's bringing Bananas to my island.' He looked at
them very sternly, then in a slow deliberate voice, 'I will
not have bananas on my island. Do you hear.' And then
shouting 'NO BANANAS ON MY ISLAND. NOW GO!
GO FIND HIM! STOP HIM!' He watched as the

Admiral and the Captain bumped into each other as they rushed for the door. 'NO BANANAS ON MY ISLAND' echoed through the corridors of the palace as they hurried to their respective posts.

Jim continued to scan the horizon, always on the lookout. He shouted up to monkey again. 'Anything on the horizon Monkey?' From the top of the middle mast Monkey could see for miles and miles and should be able to see any of the Princes ships before they got too close.

A banana skin landed on top of Jim's head. Monkey had taken a liking to bananas. He shouted up, 'Monkey, will you stop eating all the bananas.' He heard a series of OO OO OO's and AA AA Aa's, which in monkey language meant, 'I'm a monkey, what did you expect.' But Jim couldn't understand that.

They sailed quietly zig zagging across the sea when all of a sudden Monkey started to squeal and jump and swing around excitedly. In Monkey language this meant something but Jim didn't really know what. But Monkey was pointing to a spot on the horizon and Jim knew what that meant. That spot might just be one of the Princes ships coming to stop him. But Jim had a plan. Jim always had a plan.

With three masts the Jolly Nana was the fastest ship on the sea. He could easily outrun this navy ship but with a full load of Bananas onboard Jim didn't want to go out of his way. He had to go past this ship. 'Changing ship.' Jim shouted up to Monkey. Jim pulled on levers and pully's that had been installed in Jeremiah's dock yard and slowly the middle mast and sails lowered and folded down onto the deck. A pull on another lever and wooden walls and a roof popped up to hide them. And then another lever rotated the name plates on the bow and stern and she became The Traveling Trudger. Now his ship looked like an old slow traders ship. Not the fast smugglers ship the Princes Navy were looking for.

Jim and Monkey watched as the spot grew larger. Sails came into view then as the ship got closer they could see the flag, it was a Navy ship. As it got closer and closer they could see the Captain looking at them through his telescope. Jim and Monkey ignored the Navy ship, pretending not to care, pretending that they had nothing to hide. They just sat on their chairs on the poop deck and watched as the Navy ship approached.

On the Navy ship the Captain was asking his First Mate. 'Is it them? Is it them do you think?' The First Mate was scanning Jim's ship through his telescope. 'No sir. It doesn't look like them. It's only got two masts and looks like an old trading ship. Far too slow for the smuggler'. 'Aye, I think you right,' the Captain replied. 'Resume course Number One.'

'Aye aye sir.' Turning to the crew who were all on the deck hoping for a feast of Bananas he shouted, 'Five degrees to Port. Resume the lookout. Sorry lads. It's not them. No Bananas for us today.' Grumbling, the crew resumed their duties and the ship turned away.

Jim and Monkey watched as the navy ship turned and sailed by. 'We'll wait until he is out of sight and then hoist our middle mast again,' Jim said. 'Another day and we'll be there.'

Slowly the ships parted. One of the lookouts on the Navy ship watched through his telescope as Jim's ship began to fade into the distance. 'What!' he said with surprise. The setting sun was lighting a trail of yellow octopuses floating on the water, following Jim's ship. 'What!' The lookout said again. And then, 'Octopuses aren't yellow. Octopuses don't float. But if they're not octopuses then they must be, . . . banana skins. BANANAS' he shouted. 'Banana skins are following that ship.'

All telescopes turned towards Jim's ship and as the Captain saw the yellow trail of banana skins he screamed. 'We've been fooled. That was the smuggler. Number One, turnabout. Catch that ship.'

On the Jolly Nana Jim was watching. He wanted to pick up speed again and was waiting for the Navy ship to be far enough away before pulling the levers and pullies to re-hoist his middle mast. He noticed as the navy ship began to turn. 'What's going on,' he asked himself. Then something caught his eye in the water. His eyes followed the floating trail of banana skins before he realised. 'Monkey,' he shouted. He turned to look and Monkey who was sat by the rail just finishing the last of a large bunch of Bananas. He burped as he casually threw the

skin over the side. 'Monkey, you banana brain,' Jim
shouted again. 'You've given us away.' Monkey looked at
Jim and then in the direction Jim was pointing. He saw
the Navy ship turning and the trail of Banana skins he had
left. 'OOOO' he said rather sheepishly, scratching his
head.

'No time to worry.' Jim said as he began to pull the levers
and pullies. 'At least we're past him and going in the right
direction, but it's going to be harder now. We'll have to
lose him and get to the island before he can warn anyone.
It's a good job they haven't invented radio yet. At least he
can't tell anyone he's seen us.' The middle mast reached
its fully rigged position and the sails filled with wind again.
'That's it. They'll never catch us now.' Jim smiled as the
wind pushed the Jolly Nana faster and faster away from his
pursuers.

'We'll have to change our plans,' Jim said, setting course
for the harbour. Jim had a plan. Jim always had a plan.
'He'll see which way we are going and follow us. As soon
as it gets dark we'll change course. There's a good place to
hide the ship on the other side of the island but it means
we will have to trek through the jungle and past the
volcano.'

They sailed on, getting further and further away from the
navy ship. As soon it was too dark for the Navy ship to
see, Jim pulled on levers and pullies and turned the big
wheel that steered the ship. The ship turned and once Jim
was happy he was on the right course, he set off to walk to
the bow. He wanted to see if he could see the lights from
any other ships. He didn't want to run into another Navy

ship by accident.

As he walked along the deck he slipped. He screamed as his feet flew out from under him, up and over his head which cracked down on the deck followed by the rest of his body Crumpled in a big heap he opened his eyes and looked straight up at the night sky. He wasn't sure if the stars he could see were real or just buzzing around in his head. Then there was a slap on his face and everything went black.

Jim reached up and pulled the great big banana skin off his face. He slowly got up. 'Monkey!' Jim shouted. Monkey was back at his post at the top of the middle mast, eating another big bunch of bananas. Jim looked up and dodged another banana skin as it came down. 'Monkey.' He shouted again. 'Stop eating all the bananas, and be careful where you drop the skins.' Monkey looked down, confused. He let out a series of OO's, EE's and Brrrr's, which in monkey language meant, 'I like bananas. But you said I can't drop the skins in the water and now I can't drop them on the deck. What do you want me to do with them?' It is probably a good job that Jim couldn't understand Monkey or he might have told him. Rubbing the bump that was beginning to grow on his head Jim continued towards the bow

EIGHT

Next morning the Jolly Nana was in a small bay on the far side of the island, moored next to an outcrop of rock that was shaded by overhanging trees. Jim had disguised the ship with branches and foliage from the jungle and pulled more branches from nearby tree's around the masts. He and monkey were busy unloading the bananas and putting them onto four wheeled carts. 'There's not as many as we set off with,' Jim said. Monkey looked back at Jim. He smiled in a strange monkey like way but made no monkey noise. But he did have a very full tummy.

After working very hard they were ready to set off. 'Monkey, climb to the top of the trees to see if you can see anybody.' This was where Monkey liked it best, in the trees and in a few seconds he was at the top of the highest tree. He looked around carefully and looking out to sea screeched a warning and pointed. Jim looked and saw a Navy ship sailing some distance from shore.

He watched the ship for a little while and as it sailed past he called up. 'He hasn't seen us. Can you see anything else?' Monkey looked around again. He could see the tops of lots of trees. He could see the volcano that screened this side of the island but he couldn't see any soldiers. Climbing back down he shrugged his shoulders. Jim took this to mean that there were no soldiers about. That wasn't unusual. Nobody came to this part of the island since it was cut off by the lava flow from the volcano's last eruption. Which was exactly why Jim had come here.

'Come on then. Let's go.' With all the carts tied together, Jim pulled the rope with a great heave and with monkey pushing behind the carts began to move. Pulling and pushing and pulling some more, they slowly made their way through the jungle. It was hot and sticky and hard work as Jim had to keep clearing the way. The old path had started to become overgrown since the islanders stopped using it.

'We'll rest here for a while,' Jim said as they came to the edge of the jungle. Jim looked out across the black undulating lava that had flowed down from the volcano. It looked as though there was no way to get the carts across. But Jim had a plan. Jim always had a plan.

There were long areas where the lava had cooled to form flows smooth enough for the carts to ride over. All Jim had to do was follow these for as long as he could until he had to change direction. But first he had to get his carts up and onto the lava. Taking some long planks from the sides of the carts he made a ramp so they could push the carts up. Once there he would use the planks to cross areas where the lava was too rough and to get him from one smooth flow to the next.

'Monkey,' Jim shouted again. 'Up to the tree-tops. See if you can see anything before we leave the jungle. Once we're out there we have nowhere to hide.' 'OO OO OO,' Monkey replied, and taking another bunch of bananas with him was soon at the top of the trees. He looked very carefully at the bananas wondering which one to eat first. Had he looked as carefully out across the lava he might have noticed the heads of the soldiers moving about in the distance. But he didn't. He was too busy munching his bananas.

Jim waited. 'Can you see anything?' he called up. There was no reply but a banana skin came tumbling down from above, then another, and another. 'Monkey.' Jim shouted. 'What have I told you about eating all the bananas.' Shortly after, Monkey came down and shrugged his shoulders. 'Good,' said Jim. 'Nobody about. Come on let's go.'

With a few big heaves and a push they got the carts up and onto the first smooth flow. They trundled along, zig zagging from flow to flow using the planks to cross the dips and delves the lava had left when it solidified. It was quite a while since the volcano had erupted but it was still quite warm on the lava. Jim wasn't quite sure if it was heat from the volcano or heat from the sun. But that didn't really matter. It was heat and heat wasn't good for his bananas. They were almost ripe and he had to get them sold before they turned brown.

'Shhh! What's that?' Jim whispered to Monkey. He thought he heard voices in the distance. Luckily they were behind a large flow that shielded them from the direction the voices had come from. Jim peeped over the top. In the distance he could see soldiers and they were coming his way. Jim looked at his bananas. A bright yellow glow in the black lava landscape. The soldiers would see them easily once they were in sight. But Jim had a plan. Jim always had a plan. From one of the carts he took several big black sheets. 'Quick,' he said to Monkey. 'Help me cover the carts. The black sheets will camouflage the bananas.' Very quickly the bananas were covered and Jim and monkey slipped under the sheet covering the last cart, watching and waiting.

A soldier appeared around the end of the flow, then another and another. Soon a platoon of soldiers were all standing, looking around. 'I'm sure I thought I saw something,' Jim heard one of them say. 'You must have been in the sun for too long,' another replied. 'There's nothing here. Where would you hide a load of bananas. You'd be able to see them from miles away,' 'It is hot out here,' another soldier joined in. 'You might have seen the sun reflecting off the lava.' But the corporal in charge wasn't too sure. He scratched his chin, thinking. 'Perhaps it was a reflection,' he said. 'Or perhaps not.'

Jim and Monkey looked at each other under the black sheets. 'Oh dear,' Jim whispered. 'He seems suspicious. Perhaps we haven't fooled him. If they discover us run back to the jungle and to the ship. We'll have to leave the bananas.'

The corporal continued to look around, all the while scratching his chin. 'There's nothing here,' he said finally. 'But Jim is crafty.' He paused thinking, still scratching his chin. 'He's managed to fool us all before but he won't fool me again.' 'I like bananas,' one soldier said. 'So do I,' said another. 'BUT OUR PRINCE DOES NOT.' The corporal screamed. 'He doesn't like bananas and they are banned from the island. IS THAT CLEAR?' 'Yes corporal, yes corporal,' the soldiers all muttered. 'Right. It's getting late and it'll be dark soon. We'll make our way back to town but post guards between here and there to make sure he doesn't sneak through.'

The soldiers left and Jim and Monkey crawled out from under the sheets. 'Oh dear.' Jim said. 'Some soldiers will let us through for a bunch of bananas but others won't. It's going to be too risky to go that way now.' He looked towards the volcano where smoke was twisting in the wind as it rose from the crater at its summit. Jim had a plan. Jim always had a plan. 'We'll have to go through the secret tunnels in the volcano instead.'

NINE

They waited until the soldiers were out of sight then pulled back the sheets. After putting them away Jim warned, 'It'll be hot in there and we'll need to get through as fast as we can.' 'Ooo, Ee, Ah, Oo Oo Ee.' Monkey said, which in monkey language meant, 'Jim, I don't really like volcanoes very much and I don't want to go in there and get burnt.' Jim listened carefully then said. 'Monkey, sometimes I wish I could understand you and sometimes I don't, and right now I think it's better that I don't. Come on, we need to get moving.' Jim pulled on the rope and reluctantly monkey pushed from behind. The carts began to move. If Jim had looked behind as they left he might have seen the pile of banana skins they were leaving behind.

They reached the entrance to the secret tunnels just as the sun was beginning to set and the light was beginning to fade. They looked into the tunnel where an eerie red glow was coming from deep within the volcano and reflecting off the walls and the vapours that filled the air. They could hear the dull roar and feel the heat from red hot molten magma that was rushing around in deep subterranean rivers and the whole volcano seemed to creak.

Jim had explored the tunnels before so knew what to expect. But Monkey was very afraid. 'Stay close to me and do as I say,' Jim said. 'It looks and sounds worse than it is. But do be careful not to let the carts slip. Some of the paths have quite a slope towards pits that fall into the magma. We don't want to lose any bananas.' This didn't help monkey very much. He was still afraid. This wasn't one of Jim's better plans. To help get over his fear he ate some more bananas.

They made their way into the volcano. Pulling and pushing and staying as far away as they could from the pits where the magma could be seen bubbling and hissing in the bottom. Sometimes the tunnel split into two or more passages but Jim always seemed to know which way to go. But Monkey wasn't sure and thoughtfully left a trail of banana skins just in case he needed to find his own way back.

Entering a large cavern with a huge magma pit in the middle they stopped. 'We need to be careful here,' Jim said. The path was narrow and had quite a slope towards the pit. 'We'll have to take the carts two at a time so we don't lose control.' Jim untied every other cart and together they pushed and pulled the first pair carts past the pit to the other side. Then the second pair. The third pair was a bit more difficult. One had a wobbly wheel that had been damaged on the lava flows and try as they might they just couldn't stop it from running towards the pit pulling the other with it. They struggled and struggled until both carts were so close to the edge they were in danger of rolling over. Jim quickly cut the ropes that tied them together. 'Better to lose one than both,' Jim said as the cart tippled over the edge and down into the magma. There was a great splash of red-hot sparks and molten rock as the cart hit the bottom. The whole cavern seemed to groan and creak and a great cloud of steam that strangely smelt of bananas filled the air.

Jim and Monkey worked even faster now. They got the cart to the other side and worked until there were only four left. The cart at the back was the lightest as it now had only half the bananas it started with. 'Monkey. You greedy little ape.' Jim said. Monkey looked at Jim expecting him to be angry but a half smile on Jim's face gave him away. Jim didn't really mind Monkey eating some bananas.

Just then they heard voices coming from the tunnel they had just come down. 'Look, here's another one,' they heard someone call. The corporal had come back with some of his soldiers and found the pile of banana skins Monkey had left behind. Then they followed the trail to the entrance and then through the tunnels. 'Quick,' Jim said, cutting the ropes to the last cart. Leaving it at the entrance they pulled the remaining three into the middle of the cavern. They stopped while Jim placed a plank under the wheels of the third cart to stop it rolling into the magma pit then he cut it's ropes and leaving it behind pulled the last two all the way through.

Making sure the carts could not be seen Jim and Monkey hid behind boulders and watched as the soldiers appeared on the other side of the cavern. 'Ooh look,' one called out excitedly as he found the first cart. 'A cart full of bananas.' 'Yes. Come on. Let's go,' the corporal shouted. 'They can't be far ahead.' 'No no,' the others protested. 'We can't just leave the bananas here.' 'Well we can't take them with us,' the Corporal insisted. 'Well! We'll just have to eat them,' the soldier said. 'Yeh, we'll eat them,' the others agreed. The corporal tried hard to get his men to move on but they were all busy peeling bananas. The Corporal let out a sigh as he accepted the banana one of his men was holding out for him. Jim smiled as he watched. Reaching down he picked up the end of a rope and gave it a tug. He had tied the other end to the plank under the wheels of the cart left in the middle of the cavern.

The soldiers were all too busy eating bananas to notice the cart as it rolled over the edge, down into the magma below. Just as before, there was a great splash of hot sparks and magma as the cart hit the bottom. The whole cavern groaned and creaked and a great cloud of banana smelling steam filled the air. The soldiers screamed. 'Run. Run. It's erupting.' Jim placed his hand over Monkey's mouth to stop him laughing as the soldiers ran back the way they had come. Jim's plan had worked but the volcano was now beginning to make some very strange rumbling noises. 'Come on,' he said. 'I think we need to get out of here.'

Jim and Monkey pushed and pulled again through more and more tunnels until they emerged on the other side of the volcano, thankfully breathing the fresh air. They stood watching for a short while catching their breath and cooling down. Before them lay more lava flows with the jungle beyond and beyond that, through the darkness, they could see the lights of the town. Pulling and pushing again they crossed the lava flows and were soon in the jungle. They quickly made their way through the undergrowth getting closer and closer to Jim's chosen spot.

Once there they hid the carts with leaves and bushes and leaving Monkey standing guard a very ugly woman went into the town. She had several people she needed to call on and they would spread the word. By morning everyone would know where to go and what to do to get their bananas.

TEN

In the Palace the corporal was telling the Prince about their narrow escape in the volcano while chasing the banana smuggler. 'We only just escaped with our lives. My men were exceptionally brave.' He decided not to tell that they had stopped to eat some bananas.

'CALL OUT THE GUARD.' The Prince shouted. 'POST EXTRA GUARDS AT ALL GATES'. NO BANANAS CAN COME INTO THIS TOWN. FIND HIM. GET THOSE BANANAS OFF MY ISLAND.' He waved his fingers in the air screaming. 'OFF MY ISLAND.'

Soldiers ran and scurried everywhere. The guard was doubled on all gates. 'What will you do if you catch someone with Bananas?' one soldier asked another. 'I don't really know,' the other replied. 'It's been so long since I've seen one I've forgotten what they look like. How can I stop people from bringing bananas in when I don't know what they look like. And anyway, my wife is going to get some and if I try to stop her I really will be in trouble.' 'So is mine,' the first soldier grinned. They both laughed quietly.

In the jungle Jim and Monkey waited. As dawn broke people started to move about in the streets. They had been told to be very quick to get their bananas before they were all gone and before the Special Banana Guard could realise what was going on.

There was a lot of activity at the gates that led out to the fields but that was normal. People went to work in the fields every day. But the gates on one side of the town had a little more activity than normal. 'Where are you going?' The guards would ask the people. 'Were going to the jumble sale,' was the standard reply. A reason was needed for so many people going in and out of the gates on one side of the town and Jim had thought a jumble sale was a very good reason.

People started to arrive at Jim's cart's and he was selling his bananas very quickly. The people carried them back in baskets, hidden under other fruits and produce. Try not to look suspicious Jim instructed. If you look suspicious the guards will probably stop you. If you look natural and normal they probably won't.

Jim also had some other helpers that had come out from the town. To these he gave jumble wrapped in cloth. 'Look suspicious as you go through the gates and streets,' he instructed. 'As though you have something to hide. The guards will stop and search you and leave the people with bananas alone.' It seemed like a good plan. Jim always had a plan.

At first everything seemed to be working well but the Captain of the Special Banana Guard was suspicious. They had stopped several people carrying suspicious looking bundles but all they had found was jumble. 'Something's going on,' the Captain said. Leading his men they followed the crowd to the busy gates.

The Captain watched very carefully. He could see people crossing the fields that surrounded the town. This was not unusual as many people worked in the fields, but something was very odd. 'Lots of people are coming and going from over there,' he said pointing to a spot across the fields. 'Yes. There's a jumble sale going on,' one of the guards at the gate said. The Captain looked at the guard in disbelief. 'How could you be so stupid,' he said. 'Come on men.' The Captain set off with his men following, heading towards the where Jim was selling the last of his bananas.

Monkey, who was on look out at the top of a tree, began to EE EE EE and OO OO OO and jump up and down pointing. Jim knew Monkey was trying to tell him something but even though he couldn't understand what he was saying Jim knew what that meant.

'Come on Monkey, time to go,' he shouted. 'That way quickly. Pull these carts behind you.' Jim had been prepared for the guard coming and had a plan. Jim always had a plan.

The carts trundled away and quickly disappeared. Very soon after the Captain and his men burst through the jungle and into the clearing. 'I knew it. I knew it,' the Captain shouted. It was clear that many people had been there but all were now gone.

The Captain looked around and examined the ground, he quickly discovered tracks left by the the carts. 'Ah! They went that way,' he shouted. 'Come on. We have him now.' With the Captain leading the guards all charged into the jungle following the tracks. Without heavy carts to pull they would soon catch up.

After a short run they stopped. The tracks split into two different directions. One set turning into the fields and the other continuing through the jungle. 'He's trying to trick us,' the Captain said. 'He thinks that we'll think that he's stayed in the jungle, so he'll have gone into the fields.' He paused for a moment. 'But then he'll think that we'll know that, so he'll have stayed in the jungle.'

The Captain looked confused. 'So what shall we do?' one of his men asked. 'You men follow the tracks through the fields,' the Captain ordered some of his men. 'We'll follow these track through the jungle. I'm not letting him escape this time.' The Guard split into two squads and each followed a set of tracks.

Jim and Monkey were making good progress. But so where the Captain and his men. 'I can hear them,' the Captain said as the sound of cartwheels bumping across the ground came through the foliage.

Going faster now the Captain and his men soon surrounded the cart. The back of the cart was still loaded and covered in a big black sheet. Proudly the Captain strutted towards the two hooded figures at the front of the cart. I have you now,' he said and with a smile gestured to his men to pull the sheet off to reveal the bananas.

'WHAT! WHAT! WHAT'S THIS!' the Captain shouted as the sheet fell to the floor. 'Melons.' One of the figures said pulling back his hood to reveal that he was just one of the field workers. 'We've been harvesting melons and we bought one of these carts from the jumble sale to take them back to the town.

'Noooooooo.' The Captain cried. 'No No No No No.'

In the bay on the far side of the island Jim and Monkey were just clearing the last of the branches and foliage away from the ship. They had gone in the opposite direction to the carts and followed the coast path back to the ship. 'I wonder if Captain Stupid has found any of our carts yet' he said, feeling rather pleased with himself.

Jim cast off and pushed the ship away from the side. Pulling on levers and pullies the sails unfurled and filled with wind that pushed the Jolly Nana out to sea.

The Prince watched from his balcony as a ship with three masts appeared from around the headland and continue on it's way out to sea. 'Is that him? Is that him?' he asked again. 'Why didn't my guard catch him? Why isn't my Navy chasing him? WHY HAS EVERYBODY LET ME DOWN?' he finally cried. There was no answer. All of his guards and servants had gone home for lunch.

The Prince wandered down the corridor and down some steps to the kitchen. Only one person remained. 'Cook, what's for lunch?' the Prince demanded. 'Ehm! I've made some sandwiches with, Ehm, Ehm,' cook faltered, looking for words. 'And for dessert, I have made some custard with, Ehm, Ehm.' 'It had better not be bananas,' the Prince said, looking at the cook sternly, and then at the top of his voice he screamed. 'I DON'T LIKE BANANAS!'

The cry echoed through the empty corridors of the palace and out across the water. It reached the ears of Jim and Monkey who were watching over the stern as the Jolly Nana sailed further and further away from the island. 'I don't think the Prince likes bananas,' Jim said smiling. Monkey looked up at Jim with an OO and an EE and handed him a banana. 'Yes, it is a long way home my little friend.' Jim said. 'I knew you would keep some for the journey. Thank you.'

As the island disappeared over the horizon, Jim sent Monkey back to the top of the middle mast to have a look around. Monkey gave Jim the signal that nothing could be seen and once happy that nobody was watching Jim pulled a few levers and pullies and spun the big wheel that steered the Jolly Nana. The ship responded with a turn. Jim began his zig zag course back to the secret island.

He settled down on his seat on the poop deck and munched on a few bananas Monkey had left for him. He had some thinking to do. Jim needed some new plans. For the next time.

ELEVEN

A day and a night later, Jim walked up to the poop deck as the sun rose over the horizon. Monkey was already at the top of the middle mast. 'Can you see anything?' Jim called up. Monkey rubbed his eyes and looked around. Jim was stretching the night stiffness out of his body when Monkey started screeching. Looking up to see which direction Monkey was pointing Jim grabbed his telescope but he didn't need it. He could see the sail very clearly, no, not one sail, lots of sails. And they were close, too close and they were getting closer. Thought's raced round Jim's mind. 'How have they got here? I'm sure I left them well behind. How did they know where I am? Looking carefully now he could make out seven ships. One large ship in the centre with lots of ornate flags flying from its masts and rigging escorted by six galleons, two on either side and one to front and rear.

Looking through his telescope he could see that the two nearest galleons had turned towards him and were getting their canons ready. He looked at the stern where the ensign would be flying. This would tell him if they were the Princes ships. 'No. Not the Prince's navy,' Jim saw with some relief but who's, and they were still getting canons ready. 'This could mean trouble,' Jim thought wondering if the Prince had got somebody to help him.

They were still out of canon range but getting closer. Jim pulled on some levers and pullies then reached for the big wheel that steered the ship. As the ship turned he reached for the secret compartment and pulled the lever inside. The big flaps on the sides of the ship opened and the great booms swung out then up. The rigging swung out from the booms and the sails unfurled and filled with wind.

Jim watched as the Jolly Nana began to pick up speed. He was expecting the galleons to try and catch him or to change course and try to cut him off. But instead they turned and resumed their original position in the flotilla. He breathed a sigh of relief as he saw the cannon crew's standing down. 'Strange,' he thought. 'They weren't after me at all. They were just protecting the big ship in the middle. I wonder who it is?

Pulling the secret lever again the extra sails and booms folded back into their compartments and the ship resumed its normal appearance. Jim watched and waited until the flotilla was on the horizon before zig zagging his way back onto his original course. He had to be careful not to let the flotilla see which way he was really going.

Arriving back at the secret island Jim skilfully piloted the Jolly Nana back into the bay. He spent the next week tending to his trees, waiting until it was time to go back to Buba to get Jeremiah. After a long day on his plantation Jim sat in the shade next to the shack enjoying a meal and a drink. From here he could see the bay where the Jolly Nana was moored. But he sat up with a jump when another ship came into view, slowly manoeuvring into the bay. Jim looked at the ship carefully. It wasn't one of the Princes ships and it wasn't a galleon. Who could it be? But Jim had a plan, Jim always had a plan.

He got up and went quickly to his first position. He and Jeremiah had thought they might be discovered one day and had lots of booby traps ready. The ship came to a stop in the middle of the bay and dropped anchor. Jim's hand hovered above the lever, waiting for the right moment. A small boat with only one man swung out and began to lower into the water. Instead of pulling the lever Jim smiled. It wasn't Jeramiah, it was Jeramiah's man from Buba.

Jim met the boat on the beach and helped the man ashore. 'I have some important news from Jeremiah,' he said. Giving the man some food and drink they settled down. Jim listened very carefully to the news and instructions the man had brought. 'I need to get going,' the man said as the sun set. 'I can go east in the dark and then turn straight back to Buba on the dawn. Jeremiah needs me back as quick as I can.'

Next morning Jim got busy and after a day's hard work he was ready. With the Jolly Nana loaded with the best bananas he had grown he set off, bound for Buba. The journey was uneventful but as he approached Buba Jim was intercepted by two galleons, both with their cannons loaded and pointing at him. Jim wasn't concerned. He had been told that this would happen. As he entered the harbour another galleon with cannons at the ready stood between him and the flotilla flag ship moored at the royal berth. Jim tied up at one of the trading berths as instructed. Jeremiah was there to meet him.

'What's this all about?' Jim asked as he walked down the gang plank to meet his old friend. 'I'll tell you later but have you brought what I asked?' Jeremiah asked anxiously. 'Yes, of course,' Jim replied. 'I'll need to get busy unloading to take them to the market.' 'Leave that, my men will see to it. Just show them where the special ones are. We're taking them with us.' Confused, Jim did as Jeremiah asked and soon they were walking along the dock side with a man pushing the cart behind them. 'That's a very fine ship,' Jim said looking at the flag ship. 'Indeed it is,' Jeremiah agreed. 'And it belongs to a very important person.'

Back in Jeremiah's office Jeremiah explained. 'The ship belongs to the Queen of Hinglend. Hinglend is a very important country on the other side of the big sea. She's here on a tour of the Currybean islands and she's stopped here for a while. I got talking to a Captain from one of the galleons and he told me about a ship they had come across on the way here. He said as they turned to challenge this ship it turned away and was so fast they would never have caught it, even if they had wanted too. I knew straight away it was you. I told them it was one of my ships and as a result of that I have been invited to a banquet that the King is holding tomorrow in honour of the Queen.'

'Wow,' Jim said trying to take it all in. 'That's all very nice, but what's that got to do with me.' Jeremiah smiled. 'Because your going to serve your bananas at the banquet. Your going to the palace kitchen to show the cooks how to prepare the best banana deserts ever. I know you can do it. It's all arranged.' Jim was lost for words but a couple of hours later he was in the palace kitchen teaching the cooks all about bananas and how to prepare the most delicious deserts.

Next day Jim was on the market selling his bananas to the people. But he was anxious. How were the cooks doing?

Were they doing it as he had shown them? If they got it wrong it could be a disaster.

When the market closed Jim went back to Jeremiah's office and waited. It was very late in the evening when Jeremiah returned. 'How did it go?' Jim asked of his friend even before Jeramiah had taken his coat off. 'Relax.' Jeremiah assured Jim. 'Sit down and I'll tell you all about it. The banquet itself was as you would expect.' 'Really,' Jim said, perplexed. 'What would I expect? I've never been to a banquet.' Jeremiah realised his mistake. 'No of course not, sorry. Anyway. The table was lavishly laid out with all kinds of food and fruit and right in the middle was a platter of bananas arranged in patterns to show them off at their very best.' 'Ah! Yes. I showed the cooks the best way to do it,' Jim said with some relief. Jeremiah continued, 'The Queen saw them but didn't seem to take any notice and I was too far away to draw her attention to them. The meal was served and I was starting to get a little anxious.' Jim sat with concern all over his face. 'Then the desert came out,' Jeremiah paused, taking great pleasure at the look on Jim's face. 'Yes yes,' Jim said, urging his friend on. 'It was a masterpiece, a work of art, better than anything you've done before.' Jim clasped his hands in delight. 'Yes! The palace cooks showed me a few tricks as well.' 'Well it worked,' Jeremiah added. 'It tasted even better than it looked and the Queen was bowled over. She loved it.' Jim jumped up and started to dance and sing. 'Yes, yes, yes yes yes.' He paced up and down for some seconds taking it all in, then stopped. 'So. Now what?' He asked. 'We've made a nice banana desert for some Queen from somewhere across the big sea but how does that help us?

A wide grin spread across Jeremiah's face. 'Because Jim lad, once she'd tasted them she wanted to know more about them. She asked the King if they were grown on his island. He said no a man from Grenana brings them in. The Queen immediately called to her secretary to put a visit to Grenana on the tour route.' 'But that's wrong,' Jim said. 'They don't come from Grenana anymore.' 'I know, but the King doesn't. I have to keep the secret island a secret even from him, and that's why we need to get to Grenana before the Queen does.' Jim's blinked several times as his mind worked. 'So, the queens going to Grenana, looking for bananas that aren't there and we have to get there before she does. Then what?' Jeremiah looked at his friend. 'That's where you come in Jim lad. You need a plan. I'll talk to some of the Captain's tomorrow. They'll tell me when they expect to arrive so we can time our arrival perfectly. By then I'm sure you'll have worked something out.'

Jim slept fitfully that night. Tossing and turning as plan after crazy plan wound and mingled through the tunnels of his dreams but by the time he woke the seed of a plan had formed in his mind. He was quiet over breakfast, Jeremiah watched, saying nothing, he knew not interrupt Jim's thought processes. 'Got it,' Jim finally said. 'I know what we need to do.'

TWELVE

Later that day Jeremiah went to see the Queens secretary
and offered to send one on his ships to Grenana in
advance of the Queen to give the Prince time to prepare.
The secretary was pleased to accept, he would have needed
to send one of his galleons but didn't want to deplete the
Queens escort. 'I'm told there's a pirate active in the
waters down there,' he told Jeremiah. Jeremiah's eyebrows
lifted in surprise. 'Really,' he replied. 'Oh, I don't think
he'll be a problem.'

The following day a ship was dispatched to Grenana and
the day after that the Jolly Nana also left harbour. Five
days later the Queens flotilla left Buba, bound for
Grenana.

After stopping off at the secret island to pick some of his
best bananas Jim set sail again. He had changed the name
on the Jolly Nana to the Yellow Supplier. He set course
for Grenana but not under full sail, he had to keep his
speed and course just right. 'Monkey,' he shouted. Keep a
sharp lookout, we're doing things a bit different and I
don't want to be taken by surprise.' A screech came down
from the top of the middle mast which Jim hoped meant
OK.

The first two days were uneventful but on the third day
Monkey began to screech and jump up and down. Jim
looked up and saw that Monkey was pointing behind
them. Picking up his telescope Jim scanned the horizon, a
ship, no, two ships, no, three ships. Jim thought for a
moment, Jeremiah had told him to stay on this course at

this speed no matter what. 'Keep an eye on them Monkey,' he shouted up. Jim kept looking behind and over the next few hours the ships got closer and closer. Even without his telescope he could make out the Queen's flag ship at the centre. The flotilla was on the same course as Jim and as they came into full view Jim noticed the two lead galleons hoist more sail. They picked up speed and the distance between them began to shrink even more quickly. Monkey began to screech and jump up and down even more as the two ships separated, obviously meaning to pass Jim one on either side, putting Jim between their cannons. But Jim held his speed and course. 'Calm down Monkey,' he shouted up. This was what Jeremiah had told him to do but he hadn't mentioned this bit. Jim was worried. 'What if this wasn't part of Jeremiah's plan.'

The bow of one ship came close to Jim's stern. 'Ahoy Jim lad,' he heard. Jim looked to see Jeremiah waving from the bow. Jim breathed a massive sigh of relief before waving back. 'Fall in behind the ships to the rear,' Jeremiah shouted again. 'You know what to do once we get to Grenana.' As the flotilla passed Jim hoisted more sail to keep up. To all appearances the Yellow Supplier was now part of the Queens flotilla.

On Grenana Jeremiah's man had arrived and gone to see the Prince. 'The Queen of Hinglend is on a tour off the Currybean islands,' he explained. The Prince became very excited and listened very carefully before barking out orders.

'Prepare the V.I.P guest quarters. Clean the palace from

top to bottom. Prepare a royal berth for her ship. Clean the streets. Tell the fisherman to get washed, tell the market people to get washed. Tell everybody to get washed. And prepare a banquet. Employ more staff if you need too.' People began to scurry about everywhere and the preparations began. The Prince called for the Captain of the Special Banana Guard. 'Captain, that vagabond Jim might try to take advantage of this visit and try to smuggle bananas onto my island. You had better make sure he doesn't succeed.'

A few days later the flotilla arrived. The Queens ship tied up at the royal berth while the galleons formed a protective guard around the harbour. Anchored behind the galleons was the flotillas supply ship, the Yellow Supplier. The Prince stood on the quay side ready to greet the Queen. 'That ship looks familiar,' he said to the Captain of the Special Banana Guard, pointing out to the Yellow Supplier. 'I thought the same your Majesty. But it arrived with the flotilla and appears to be their supply ship. Not even Jim could manage that. But I've posted guards right around the island. There is nowhere he can sneak ashore and this ship is right in front of us. I'll have men watching it night and day.' 'Good. I'm relying on you Captain. Jim must not spoil this visit.'

The Queen appeared at the top of the gangway and was met with a grand fanfare of trumpets. As she stepped onto the quay the Prince took her hand and escorted her to the state carriage, a horse guard to front and rear. The procession left the harbour and passed through the streets on its way up to the palace. Islanders lined the route and cheered and clapped as they passed, or else.

As soon as the procession left the harbour the real work began. The Queens servants began to unload trunks containing everything she would need during the visit. There were lots of trunks and as they came off the ship they were stacked on the quayside. This was a reason the Queen had the biggest ship in the flotilla. Carts arrived, the trunks were loaded and a relay began to take everything up to the palace.

From the Yellow Supplier a small boat slowly lowered into the water. It rowed ashore with only one person on board. The guards watched carefully. 'Wow! She's ugly,' one said as the boat approached the landing. 'We still need to check her out,' the other said. 'But let's make it quick.' They caught the rope the lady threw and tied the boat up. 'What's your business,' they demanded as the lady climbed out. 'Why, I'm one of the Queens cooks,' the ugly lady said. 'I need to get to the palace kitchen as quick as I can. I have special ingredients that the Queen demands with her food. They're in that case.' She pointed to a large chest in the boat. 'Be a good chap and lift it out for me will you.' She smiled at the guard as nicely as she could and the guard became afraid. 'Eric, get the case. Be quick,' the guard said to his companion. The ugly woman continued to smile and the guard became even more afraid. 'Where would you like your case,' he said, anxious to get this woman on her way. 'On one of the carts if you would be so kind,' she said, holding out her hand to be escorted. The two guards carried the case. The ugly woman had to walk by herself.

The cart trundled away and was soon in the palace courtyard. The ugly woman managed to lift the case off the cart and carry it to the kitchen all by herself. Cook looked at her suspiciously. 'Who are you and what do you want?' As the ugly woman explained cook was looking at her very carefully. 'I've seen you somewhere before. I know you from somewhere.' 'Oh no,' the ugly woman laughed. 'That wouldn't be possible. And even if it was you might be better off not remembering.' The final words hung in the air as the cook tried to figure out what she meant. Deciding that she might be right he pointed to a space in the kitchen as far away from where he would be as possible. 'You can work over there he said.'

On his veranda overlooking the sea, the Prince was talking to the Captain of the Special Banana Guard. 'Are you sure,' he was asking. 'Yes your majesty. I have guards all around the coast, the Admiral has his ships stationed all around the island and with the Queens galleons guarding the harbour there is nowhere he can sneak ashore.' 'Good.' The Prince said with some satisfaction. 'The Queens banquet is tomorrow and nothing can be allowed to spoil it.'

Next day everything was ready. The table was laid with the best silver and china and the Princes servants dared not to get even the slightest detail wrong. The banquet began, the Prince was nervous, he wanted so much to impress this important Queen. 'You have done well,' she commented. 'Why thank you ma'am,' the Prince replied proudly. 'Yes, the King of Buba spoke highly of your island,' the Queen added. 'We do our best,' the Prince responded hiding his confusion. 'Why would the King of Buba mention my island,' he thought. The servants arriving with food cut through the Princes thoughts. The meal was exceptional. 'Cook has really done well,' the Prince thought. 'But why can't he do it this well all the time. I need to have words with him.'

With the main course over the table was prepared for dessert. The servants entered carrying platters filled with the best fruit grown on the island. They placed them on the table and right in the middle, a platter filled with perfectly arranged bananas. The Princes eyes went wild and his nostrils flared as he took a deep breath ready to scream out. 'Are you quite well?' the Queen enquired. 'Oh. Yes, yes,' the Prince replied regaining his composure. 'My apologies ma'am. I was stifling a sneeze.' More servants arrived with the desert. 'Ahh My favourite,' the Queen said with delight as a bowl of exquisitely prepared banana surprise was placed in front of her. The Princes jaw dropped and began to wobble as his desert was placed in front of him.

'This why I came here,' the Queen said. The King of Buba told me they are grown on your island.' The Princes jaw continued to wobble as the Queens words echoed inside his head. 'I would very much like to see where they are grown.' The Princes jaw stopped wobbling, he was stiff with rage, fear, confusion and pride. So many different emotions he didn't know how he felt. He looked down the table to where the Captain of the Special Banana Guard was sitting. His jaw was wobbling just as much but he had only one emotion, fear. Despite all his precautions

Jim had not only managed to get bananas onto the island, he had managed to get them served to the Queen of Hinglend at the banquet. Despite his fear he heard the Queen and saw that the Prince was speechless. 'No, I'm sorry ma'am,' he intervened. 'It's much too dangerous.' 'Oh really. Why?' The Queens replay was very direct. Thinking quickly the Captain replied, 'Snakes,' your Majesty. 'Lots and lots of snakes. We wouldn't be able to guarantee your safety.' Oh, that's a great shame. I was so looking forward to seeing how they are grown.' The Queen was disappointed. Turning back to the Prince she continued. 'My secretary will speak with yours and make some arrangements'.

The Captain made his apologies and left the table. As soon as he was through the door he ran down to the kitchen. 'Cook. Cook.' He was shouting. Cook appeared. 'Where did those bananas come from, and why, why did you serve them to the Queen, and our Prince.' 'I didn't,' the cook protested. 'One of the Queens cooks came and said she was going to prepare the queens favourite dessert. She worked over there. I couldn't see what she was doing.' 'Where is she now,' the Captain demanded. 'I don't know. She left as soon as the plates went up.' The Captain turned and ran from the kitchen. Through the courtyard, through the streets, through the market and into the harbour. Running to the end of the quay he stopped. The Yellow Supplier was pulling up its anchor and hoisting its sails. He watched as the wind took the ship out to sea and away. 'How? How? How? How?' The question just kept rolling around and around in his head.

On the Poop deck Jim and Jeremiah were talking and

laughing. 'You should have seen his face,' Jeremiah was saying. 'He just didn't know what to do. As soon as the Queen said it was her favourite I made my apologies for a toilet break and left.' 'I wish I could have seen it,' Jim replied. 'He'll be as mad as hell. This is going to change things. We won't be able to come back here for a long long time.'

THIRTEEN

A few days later the Queen and her flotilla left Grenana. The Prince stood politely waving but as soon as the ships were far enough away he let out a mighty scream had been trapped inside since the banquet.

Later in the palace the Captain of the Special Banana Guard and the Admiral stood before him. The Prince was pacing up and down muttering. 'You promised me. You promised me. You failed me. How? How?' He stopped pacing and looked sternly at the two men. 'After all your precautions he managed to get bananas onto my banquet table. How? How? How did he manage to do that? The two men said nothing.

Talking very deliberately the Prince continued. 'Now I have some instructions for you.' The Prince told the men what he wanted them to do. 'Do not fail me again. If you do, it will be the dungeon for you both. Forever. Now go. Go and find them and do what you have to do.'

The two men left to make their plans. They stood at a table with a chart of the Currybean sea laid out in front of them. 'I've had men in small boats positioned around the sea for a while now,' the Admiral explained. 'Almost impossible to see from a ship. They've been making reports and I've been plotting their sightings. I think they go somewhere around here.' He pointed to an area on the chart. 'Good.' The Captain replied. 'I'll get my men ready. You assemble your ships and we'll be on our way. And if we don't find him I'm going to live on Buba.'

With the Admiral in command, the Princes flag ship the
navy left Grenana with the rest of the navy ships joining in
formation. The Prince watched from his balcony as they
sailed away. 'You had better not fail me,' he thought.

A few days into the voyage the Admiral gave the order for
the ship to form a wide line abreast, spread out to give
them the greatest chance of finding the secret island.
Slowly they made their way North, all the time lookouts
scanning the horizon. A couple of days later one of the
ships hoisted some signal flags. All ships immediately
turned and made towards the signalling ship. As each
arrived it furled it's sails until they were all stopped in a
cluster. The Admiral sent a trusted man to the top of the
mast and waited. 'Aye aye sir,' the man shouted down.
'Dark shape on the horizon five points to the North.
Looks like it could be an island.'

The Captain from each ship went onto the flag ship for a
briefing. The Admiral examined the charts very carefully.
'There's nothing shown for an island there,' he said. 'If it
was an island it would be on the charts but what else could
it be?' What the Admiral didn't know was that it was one
of Jeremiah's companies that produced the charts and he
always made sure that the island was never shown.
Deciding that it had to be the island the Admiral assigned
duties to each of the Captains and they returned to their
ships. They waited until late into the night before hoisting
sail again. Each ship heading for its allocated position.

On the island Jim and Jeremiah were sleeping. at the top of a tree monkey was sleeping too. It was quieter up there but he could still hear Jim snoring. As dawn broke monkey stretched and carefully turned over on his branch. As he did he opened one eye to make sure he didn't fall off. But that one eye saw something that made both eyes open wide and Monkey sat bolt upright, wide awake.

The sound of monkey screeching woke both Jim and Jeremiah. 'He's making a lot of noise,' Jeremiah said as he opened his eyes. 'Must be having a bad dream,' Jim replied as he turned over. But monkey's continued screeching made both men sit up. 'Something's not right,' Jeremiah said jumping out of bed, closely followed by Jim. Running outside they looked up to the top of monkey's tree to see him jumping up and down, pointing in all directions. 'This doesn't look good,' Jim said. 'Quick, up to the platform.' Jim had built a platform in the jungle that was just at the height of the treetops. From here they could see right round the island.

After a short run and climb, they arrived at the top of the platform. They didn't need their telescopes to see the ships that were surrounding them, getting closer. One ship, the flag ship, was heading towards the bay where the Jolly Nana was moored. 'He's seen the ship,' Jeremiah said. 'Or at least seen the only place where a ship could be hidden. This is going to be tricky. We don't have time to get the ship out and away but we have about an hour. You check the traps on that side and I'll check them on this side. Make sure they're all ready and I'll meet you back here.'

Jim and Jeremiah ran as quick as they could, checking each trap as they went then met again at the top of the platform. The ships were circling the island now making sure there was no way to escape. The flag ship was getting very close to the bay. 'Hoist the flag,' Jeremiah said. 'Let battle commence.' Jim pulled on a rope and a huge scull and cross bones was raised to the top of a mast. 'That should make them wonder who they're fighting,' Jim smiled. 'You'd better go to the station in the bay,' Jeremiah said to Jim. 'We might need to use the local defences for the flag ship.' 'Good luck old friend,' Jim replied as he disappeared back down the ladder.

Jeremiah watched carefully as the ships continued their circling. He picked one. As it came within marks carefully cut into the platform handrail he pulled a lever. Down on the foreshore two trees that had been pulled back and tied with ropes were released. Free from their restraint they sprung back to their upright position pulling a huge log that flew through the air broadside on, hitting the ships rigging bring the sails crashing down.

He watched as another ship came between two similar marks. He pulled another lever and that ship suffered a similar catastrophe. One by one, each of the six ships fell into the same trap and were soon marooned without sails to push them on. That was the plan. Cripple the ships for long enough for the Jolly Nana to make its escape. But the flag ship now entering the bay was a bigger problem. The crews on the crippled ships were all busy, running around repairing the rigging and trying to pull the sails back up. Jeremiah had to give Jim enough time to do his work.

Jeremiah carefully selected his next lever. His target was in just the right place. 'Sorry boys,' he said as the lever was pulled. Another tree sprung back to its upright position, this time pulling a slingshot full of coconuts. The would-be cannon balls flew through the air raining down on the ship, bouncing around in all directions cracking the poor crew on heads, arms, ribs and shin bones. Another ship in just the right position got the same treatment.

He looked down to the bay just to see the sails of the flag ship disappear behind the trees. He didn't need to worry. Jim had the flag ship in his sights. From his position he pulled a lever and a great tree trunk was launched, again catapulted by releasing two bent back trees. This hit the flag ship right across two masts before crashing to the deck, followed by the rigging and sails. Jim could hear the Admiral shouting orders to get the deck clear. He could see the Captain of the Special Banana Guard trying to assemble his men to go ashore. 'That's what you think,' Jim thought as he pulled another lever sending a rain of coconuts down onto the deck scattering the men everywhere. He pulled another lever. A huge tree trunk came out from the foreshore, this time end on. It struck the flag ship right in the side just at the water line. Water splashed and wood splintered in all directions. As the water calmed down and the tree trunk floated free a great hole could be seen in the side of the ship, water pouring inside.

The ship started to settle lower and lower as it filled with water. The bay wasn't very deep and the ship soon hit the bottom and began roll over. Everybody and everything began to slide towards the sea with barrels rolling down the deck, knocking men into the water. The rigging and sails Jim had managed to knock down dragged men over the side. Men were splashing about everywhere making their way to the shore. Jim watched as the Admiral and the Captain of the Special Banana Guard slid down the poop deck desperately trying to grab hold of something. They hit the handrail at the same time, bounced over the top and down into the water.

Jim looked at the Jolly Nana and saw that Jeremiah was getting ready to cast of. This was part of the plan. Jim left his post and ran as fast as he could along the foreshore. Jeremiah would be ready by the time he got there. He saw the sails unfurl, a single rope now held the Jolly Nana in place, Jeremiah ready to cut it with an axe as soon as Jim was aboard. Almost there Jim heard a cry for help, his head automatically turned in the direction of the cry. The Captain of the Special Banana Guard was splashing about tangled in some of rigging that was pulling him down. Jim kept on going, then stopped, then going again, then stopped. He looked to see the man's head slowly disappear under the water. Without thinking Jim splashed into the bay then swimming as fast as he could he reached the spot where the head had slipped beneath the surface.

Jim felt something grab his leg, pulling at him, down under the water he went, grappling with the hazy figure he could just see through the murk and bubbles. Knowing he didn't have much time Jim struggled but the figure continued to pull and Jim sank deeper and deeper. Then another figure appeared in the murk. It began to bite, teeth gnashing everywhere all around the poor Captain. Then all of a sudden Jim and the Captain came free. Up they both went breaking the surface gasping for air. Jim quickly grabbed the Captain before he sank again and splashed towards the shore. Monkey splashing alongside them. Dragging the man up the beach coughing and spluttering the Captain thanked Jim over and over again. Monkey crawled onto Jim's shoulder picking bits of rope from his teeth. 'You need to thank him as much as me,' Jim said.

By now many men had managed to make it to the shore and Jim realised that his chance to escape had gone. 'I owe you my life,' he heard the Captain say. The Admiral came through the crowd of men. 'I saw what you did,' he said. 'You could have escaped but you went to save the Captain. You're a good man Jim.' Jim looked around. He was completely surrounded now. 'Yeh, well, perhaps you could return the favour and ask you men to step aside while we do escape.' 'No no. You can't,' Jim heard the Captain splutter. Jim looked at the man he had just saved. 'You don't understand,' the Captain continued. 'We didn't come here to catch you. We've brought a message, from the Prince.' 'You surrounded the island.' Jim pointed out. 'Yes of course,' the Admiral cut in. We had to stop you from escaping so we could give you the message.'

Jim thought for a moment. 'How can we trust you?' he asked. 'Men. Step aside,' the Admiral shouted. 'You are free to leave if you wish,' he gestured towards the Jolly Nana. Jim walked to the gang plank and up to the poop deck where Jeremiah had watched everything that had happened. 'What do you think?' Jim asked him. 'I don't know. He's let you come up here. We could kick the gang plank away, cut the rope and there is nothing he could do to stop us. What's the message?' 'Don't know. Didn't

ask,' Jim replied. 'What's the message?' they both shouted
down together.

'The Prince has asked for a meeting. You are both
guaranteed safe passage if you agree to meet him,' the
Admiral shouted up. Jim and Jeremiah looked at each
other. 'What have we got to lose,' Jim said. 'They know
where the island is now so were not safe here anymore.' 'I
suppose so,' Jeremiah replied thinking. 'But we have to
have the meeting on the ship. That way he can't trick us
and we have to be there before they can repair the ships
here.' They looked around the bay where the flag ship had
settled, half under water. 'We don't need to worry about
that one,' Jeremiah laughed. 'You made a right good job
of that. Very well,' he shouted down. 'We'll meet the
Prince. Would you like a lift back?' The Admiral looked
at his ship and sighed. 'That would be nice,' he said.

FOURTEEN

With no need to zig zag, the journey back was swift. They anchored just outside the harbour, not wanting to go in in case the Prince was setting a trap. The Admiral and the Captain of the Special Banana Guard rowed ashore in a boat. The Prince watched from his veranda. Shortly after, the Admiral and the Captain were stood before him. Where are they?' he asked. And where's my flag ship and where's the rest of my navy?'

Jim and Jeremiah heard him scream from the Jolly Nana. In the palace the Prince was striding up and down waving his hands above his head. 'Two men. Two men crippled my fleet and sunk my flag ship.' He stopped, looking at the two shame faced men, 'How could you. How could you have let that happen.' Walking to the veranda he looked down at the Jolly Nana anchored outside the harbour. Jim and Jeremiah were on the poop deck looking back up at the palace. Everything was ready for a quick getaway should they see any sign of treachery by the Prince. Probably for the first time in his life the Prince swallowed his pride. 'Come on then. Let's go.'

Jim and Jeremiah watched as the boat rowed back. The Prince sat, anxious but regal in the back. Jim helped the Prince up the ladder and onto the deck. He and Jeremiah both bowed, deciding it better to show the Prince some respect. The Prince was pleased to accept the gesture. Jim and Jeremiah had prepared three seats and as they sat Jim was tempted to offer the Prince a banana but thought better of it.

The meeting began. 'Jim, no matter what precautions we put in place you always managed to get your bananas onto the island and sold. And Jeremiah, you, you are the pirate.' The Prince paused shaking his head before continuing. 'You two have proved to be very resourceful and very clever and I have need of your services.' Jim and Jeremiah looked at each other. 'Go on,' they said. 'At my banquet you managed to serve a banana desert to the Queen of Hinglend,' the Prince said to Jim. The Prince smiled. 'That was clever. That was very very clever. Nobody else could have done that. And she loved it. Your bananas were the reason she came to the island in the first place.'

Turning to Jeremiah the Prince continued. 'You build the fastest ships in the world. Without doubt you are the finest naval architect there is. So, I have a proposition. The Queen of Hinglend has asked that we export our bananas to Hinglend so that she and her subjects can enjoy them there. A suitable trade deal will be set up so that we can all benefit. Jim, I would like you to return to the island and grow your bananas here. Jeremiah I will commission you to build me some ships, the fastest ships on the sea to take the bananas to Hinglend.'

The Prince sat back as Jim and Jeremiah looked at each other in disbelief. 'What if you change your mind and throw me in the dungeon once I've set up a new plantation,' Jim asked suspiciously. 'Yeh. And what if you decide not to pay me in full for the ships,' Jeremiah added. 'I give you my word,' the Prince replied, knowing the two men would have doubts. 'Once given my word cannot be broken and we will sign contracts to ensure we are all protected.' 'Excuse us,' Jeremiah said as he and Jim stood.

They walked to the back of the ship for a discussion. 'Can we trust him? Will he go back on his word? Will he tear up the contract when it suits him?' The two men had a lot to think about and they talked and thought really hard. The Prince sat watching the two men wondering what they would do.

Eventually they returned to their seats. The Prince sat and waited for them to speak. 'Very well,' Jeremiah said. 'But we want a hand in writing the contracts to make sure it's fair.' The Prince smiled, 'I agree.' And so the deal was made, contracts were written and signed. Jim returned to the island, replanted his plantation and grew the best bananas in the world. Jeremiah designed and built a fleet of ships to transport the finest Grenana bananas to Hinglend. The Queen was delighted and often had her favourite banana surprise for dessert. And the people of Hinglend were delighted when bananas appeared in shops for the very first time for them all to buy and enjoy. And that is probably why you can find bananas on your supermarket shelves to this very day.

The End

DID YOU KNOW
AMAZING FACTS ABOUT BANANAS

Bananas are good to eat, but that's not all they are good for, the skins and the plant itself all have amazing uses that you might not have known about. Read on to find out more.

Where do Bananas come from?

- It is thought that bananas were first grown for food in Southeast Asia about 7,000 to 10,000 years ago.

- Today bananas are grown in tropical regions of 120 countries around the world.

- There are about 110 different species of banana

The Banana Plant

- The banana tree isn't actually a tree. It's a plant with the 'trunk' made from layers of the stems of it's leaves. The leaves can grow to be 3 metres long and be half a metre wide.

- The banana plant is officially termed a herb and is the world's largest herbaceous flowering plant.

- A banana plant only produces one crop of bananas, after that it dies. New plants come from shoots that grow from the roots of the old plant.

- The farmer picks a shoot and let it grow to about one metre before cutting it off from its parent and replanting it where he wants it.

- A new plant takes about nine months to grow and produce a crop of bananas.

- Bananas are not only grown for their fruit. Many are grown for their fibres which are used to make paper and textiles.

- The Latin name for Banana is musa sapientum fixa. When translated it means 'fruit of the wise man'.

The Banana Fruit

- The banana fruit is technically a berry.

- Banana fruits grow in a cluster commonly called a bunch. The fruits on the bunch grow in rows called hands. There can be as many as twenty hands on a bunch. A single banana is called a finger and there can be as many as twenty fingers on a hand. How many bananas can there be on a bunch? Answer at the end of this section.

- Not all bananas are yellow, some varieties change to red or even green and white stripes.

- The bananas we buy to eat are called desert bananas.

- About 75 percent of the weight of a banana is water.

- Western cultures generally eat the soft inner part of the banana and throw the skin away. Some

Eastern cultures cook the bananas and eat both the skin and the inside.

- Bananas may also be cut and dried and eaten as a type of chip. Dried bananas are also ground into banana flour.

- Bananas are the fourth largest fruit crop in the world with more than 100 billion bananas eaten across the world every year.

- Answer. There can be as many as 400 bananas in a bunch.

Bananas are good for you

- Bananas contain vitamins C & B6, potassium, fibre and the amino acid tryptophan.

- Due to their potassium content bananas are naturally slightly radioactive, but the level of radiation is not high enough to cause harm.

- Bananas have no fat, no sodium, no cholesterol and are low in calories.

- Bananas help your body produce serotonin, a natural substance that combats depression.

Allergies

- Some people are allergic to bananas. With some people swelling starts inside the mouth or throat within an hour of eating a banana. About half of all people who are allergic to latex are also allergic to bananas and may develop a rash (hives) and tummy disorders.

Banana Handling Tips:

- Wrapping banana stems tightly in cling film will make them last three to five days longer.
- If you peel a banana from the bottom, holding onto the stem, you will avoid the stringy bits that cling to the fruit inside.
- If you put a banana in the refrigerator the peel will turn dark brown or black, but it won't affect the fruit inside.

Amazing Uses for Banana Plants

Textiles

- Fibre from the banana plant can be used to create high quality textiles.
- In Japan, people have used the fibre to create clothes and household textiles since the 13th century.
- In Nepal, the fibres are used to produce high quality rugs with a texture and general qualities similar to that of silk.

Paper

- Banana fibre is also used to make banana paper.

- There are two different kinds of banana paper, paper made from the stem fibres and paper made from the fibre from unused fruits.

Amazing Uses for Banana Skins

- Banana skins can be used to polish wooden and leather furniture and also used to polish silver.

- Banana skins can be used to remove ink from wooden or painted surfaces or from your hands.

- Bananas and banana skins make great fertiliser because of their phosphorous and potassium content. They can be composted, buried whole or cut into small pieces and mixed with garden soil. Very good for roses.

Banana Skins in First Aid

Disclaimer. This information is obtained from research on the internet and is for interest only. The author and publisher can accept no responsibility for the accuracy of this information or any ill effects suffered due to reliance on this information. Readers are advised to seek professional medical help.

Treatment for Warts

- Warts don't like the potassium in the banana skin. Rubbing the inside of a small piece of banana skin or taping it over a wart every night can make the wart disappear in one to two weeks.

Mosquito Bites & Nettle Sting

- Rub or cover the affected area with the inside of the banana skin and leave for 10-15 minutes. This will help stop the itching. *Author note! I have actually tried this on a nettle sting and trust me, any cream bought over the counter for this type of thing works far better.*

Poison Ivy Rashes

- Rub the inside of the banana skin over the rash to soothe the skin. If the skin is very sore, use the back of a knife to scrape the inside of the banana skin to remove a thick paste. Apply the paste to the affected part of the skin.

Bruises

- Tape some banana skin inside out to cover the bruise and leave overnight to help reduce discoloration and speed up healing. Rinse and dry and repeat twice or three times a day for more severe bruising.

Acne

- Banana skins contain nutrients that can calm inflamed skin and help fight inflammation and acne breakouts.
  - Rub the banana peel over your skin and leave for 5 to 10 minutes.
  - Rinse your skin.
  - Repeat twice daily.

Removing Splinters

- Banana skin is rich in enzymes that have a pulling action that will draw foreign objects to the surface of the skin making it much easier to remove with a pair of tweezers.

  o   Apply a ripe banana peel to the affected area of the skin.

  o   Leave it on the skin for 15 minutes.

  o   Gently remove it without rubbing it on the skin.

  o   Repeat until the object can be removed with tweezers.

Reduce Skin Irritations

- Banana skins contain histamine lowering nutrients such as magnesium, vitamin C, and vitamin E and are a great home remedy for itchy skin.

- Banana Skins can also drastically reduce skin irritations such as swelling, redness, and scarring.

  o   Take the banana skin and apply it to the affected area.

  o   Leave for one hour or overnight.

  o   Repeat daily.

Cuts & Abrasions

- Applying the inside of a banana skin on a scrape or burn will help the pain go away, keep the swelling down and help keep the wound from getting infected.

Migraine & Headaches

- A banana skin across the forehead and across the back of the neck can help relieve headaches.
  - o Put the banana peel in the freezer for an hour.
  - o Apply one line of skin to your forehead and one to the back of your neck.
  - o Leave it on until it becomes warm.
  - o Repeat as required.

ABOUT THE AUTHOR

Poo's real life as an engineer is very different to the imaginary lives always going in his head. Poo has worked in the North Sea, in the deserts and deep underground at CERN.

But Poo would rather tell stories. Poo has always been a storyteller. When his children were small they would sit together share adventures in his imaginary worlds. But children grow up and eventually the stories stopped. But now Poo has Grandchildren and they have given Poo a reason the bring the stories back to life.

One day during a storytelling session his granddaughter looked up at Poo and asked a very pointed question, 'Poo, are you going to get your stories made into a book?' There was expectation in that little voice. What could Poo do?

The result of that question was Poo's first book, 'A Giant Called Tiny' closely followed by The 27 Bears – The Further Adventures of Goldilox. Both pooblished by Austin Macauley and available on Amazon. This is his third book, and the expectations are still there.

Reviews are so important. Please take the time to visit the Amazon page and leave a review of the book. Poo needs to know how you liked it.

Follow Poo on Twitter: @poosbooks

Printed in Great Britain
by Amazon